*Kent Hastings knows exactly what he's looking for in a wife....*

1. "A woman who's...well...gorgeous. So how come the only woman I'm really interested in is Nellie Brown? I mean, she's attractive, I guess, but not exactly a knockout. And yet...

2. "Somebody who'll help me on my way up the corporate ladder—sleek, sophisticated, a real asset to an ambitious young executive like me. Not like *Nellie* at all. But...

3. "Somebody who's interested in the same things I am. Like Nellie, come to think of it. You know, I hardly even noticed her before, but all of a sudden she's everywhere I go. And she likes everything I do. And even though she's *completely* wrong for me, I can't quite seem to get her out of my mind...."

*Dear Reader,*

This month, wedding bells are ringing here at Yours Truly. We've got two great books all about marriage, that most wonderful of institutions. It's funny about weddings, because no matter whether the ceremony's fancy or down-to-earth, whether you know the couple well or are just meeting them for the first time, you can't help being affected by the way they love each other, can't help hoping their future will be just as wonderful as they envision. I'm going on vacation to England in a couple of weeks, and I'm going to attend the wedding of two people I've never met. And you know what? I'm going to be just as caught up in their special day as if I'd known them forever. Weddings will do that, so now join two couples *you've* never met as they figure out that yes, they really are meant to be together forever.

*Right Husband! Wrong Bride?* is the newest romance from Lori Herter. Following the advice in the book *How To Marry Your Dreamboat* has worked perfectly for Nellie—except that now she's wondering if Kent has really fallen for *her* or just for someone he thinks she is. In Jennifer Drew's *The Prince and the Bogus Bride,* the price that reporter Leigh Donovan has to pay for an interview with real-life Prince Max seems easy: pretend to be his fiancée while he's in the States, then say goodbye when he's ready to head home. The thing is, a *real* engagement is sounding better to her every minute.

Enjoy both these great books, and then come back next month for two more wonderful novels all about meeting, dating—and marrying!—Mr. Right.

Yours,

Leslie J. Wainger
Senior Editor and Editorial Coordinator

Please address questions and book requests to:
Silhouette Reader Service
U.S.: 3010 Walden Ave., P.O. Box 1325, Buffalo, NY 14269
Canadian: P.O. Box 609, Fort Erie, Ont. L2A 5X3

# LORI HERTER

*Right Husband!*
*Wrong Bride?*

SILHOUETTE YOURS TRULY™

Published by Silhouette Books
**America's Publisher of Contemporary Romance**

To my husband, Jerry, who accepts me
as I am, frills, flaws and all.

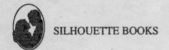 SILHOUETTE BOOKS

ISBN 0-373-52059-X

RIGHT HUSBAND! WRONG BRIDE?

Copyright © 1998 by Lori Herter

**Printed in U.S.A.**

# About the author

We all try to put our best foot forward, especially when looking for Mr. Right. I certainly did when I was single. There are even self-help books to help us learn how to present ourselves to our best advantage. But I soon realized it was no use trying to change myself to land the right man. I learned that I can only be myself—I can't be anyone else. The real secret is to find the man with whom you can be your true self, who loves you just for being who you are.

I thought this would be a fascinating issue to explore in Yours Truly. In *Right Husband! Wrong Bride?* Nellie Brown is desperate enough to win the attention of Kent Hastings, the man she loves, that she buys a book titled *How To Marry Your Dreamboat*. At first, the book's strategy seems to work. But just when her dream is within reach, Nellie begins to worry. Can Kent love the real Nellie, or is she the wrong bride for him? Read and find out....

**Books by Lori Herter**

**Silhouette Yours Truly**

*Listen Up, Lover*
*\*How Much Is That Couple in the Window?*
*\*Blind-Date Bride*
*\*Me? Marry You?*
*Right Husband! Wrong Bride?*

\* Million-Dollar Marriages

**Silhouette Romance**

*Loving Deception* #344

**Silhouette Shadows**

*The Willow File* #28

**Silhouette Books**

*Silhouette Shadows Short Story Collection* 1993
"The Phantom of Chicago"

# 1

Had it been an accident—or fate? Nellie Brown couldn't help but ponder this question as she studied the cover of the book in her hands.

A month ago, someone had clumsily brushed past her in this very aisle of the popular Chicago bookstore she regularly visited, causing her to bump against the bookshelf in back of her. A hardcover had fallen to the floor near her feet. Nellie, twenty-four, single, and in love all alone, had stared openmouthed at the book's title—*How To Marry Your Dreamboat*.

Nellie opened the now-familiar book and turned to the table of contents. She already knew all the chapter titles by heart. She'd stood in this aisle reading and rereading them many times since her first, unexpected encounter with the book. "When He Doesn't Know You Exist," and "Shyness Can Be Sexy" were the two headings that intrigued her the most. But the last chapter, "Pull In That Reel And Land Your Man," always gave her second thoughts. The self-help book sounded a little too cagey and manipulative to suit her conscience. She wasn't at all the sort of woman to go after the man she loved with a calculated scheme. No, indeed. Love ought to develop in a natural way.

But it was taking so darn long! And Kent Hastings, her own personal dreamboat, was about to be snatched from her view forever.

Nellie had worked as a staff accountant for Latham & Eliot for almost a year now, having been hired directly after graduating college and passing her C.P.A. exam. On her first day, she was introduced to Kent, a senior accountant, whose office was located near her desk. She'd been immediately impressed with his tall, slim, dark-haired good looks and his personable manner. Her first assignment was to do an audit, under his direction, of a large Chicago candy factory. Not only did she come to admire his agile business mind during the weeks they'd worked together, but also his easy sense of humor so similar to her own, and his warmth. She'd felt they'd developed a special rapport, that he'd enjoyed her company as much as she valued his. By the end of their stint at the candy factory, she'd fallen in love with him.

Unfortunately it soon had become apparent that he hadn't formed any strong, lasting attachment to her. He'd complimented her generously on her work and written her a glowing review, giving her an impressive first entry on her personnel record. But then he'd moved on to other assignments with other employees and never showed any indication that he missed working closely with her. In the many months since, she'd been assigned to work with several other senior accountants on various other audits. The personnel department, who organized the job designations, had never assigned her to work with him again. Latham & Eliot was a huge company with over fifteen hundred employees in the firm's several departments, so it was really no surprise that their work assignments hadn't dovetailed a second time.

Whenever she'd seen Kent at the office, he was friendly toward her, full of his usual cordiality and humor, yet she could not discern any difference between his graciousness toward her and any other employee. Her shy attempts to get him to notice her in particular always seemed to have failed. For example, when they'd finished the candy factory audit, she'd given him a mug filled with chocolate kisses as a way of saying she'd enjoyed working with him. He'd smiled and seemed to appreciate the gift, but it hadn't led to any reciprocal action on his part. They'd often had lunch together while working at the candy factory, but he'd never asked her to lunch since.

Now Kent was about to be promoted and she had only two weeks left to try to capture his heart. Were Nellie's scruples about the book's tactics getting in the way of her marrying *her* dreamboat?

*Bite the bullet and buy the book,* she told herself, pressing her lips together with conviction as she held the book against her chest. But by the time she had waited in line at the register, she again felt squeamish about her purchase.

"Oh, this is a popular one," the gray-haired woman behind the register said with a smile as she rang it up.

"Really?" Nellie wanted to take comfort from the fact that other customers hadn't been too scrupulous to buy it.

"We've sold tons of them." The woman handed her the credit card receipt to sign.

Nellie was so jittery she misspelled her name, leaving out an *L*. She looped one in before handing it back. "Hope it works," she told the woman.

Buttoning up her gray winter overcoat to shut out the sharp, frigid wind, Nellie walked out of the bookstore onto Wabash Avenue. She wrapped her wool scarf around her neck and covered her nose with it as she headed toward the Randolph Street skyscraper where she worked. She was overdue getting back to the office. She'd dawdled too long on her lunch hour making up her mind about the book, she thought with dismay. Was it having a bad influence on her before she'd even read it?

Ten minutes later, she walked into an elevator in the spacious lobby of her building and was pulling off her knit cap, when suddenly a tall man rushed in, pushing open the doors before they closed. Nellie silently drew in her breath. It was Kent. She held the book, wrapped in a paper bag, against her chest, self-conscious about having a guide to catching a husband in her possession while in Kent's presence. She felt so transparent.

Gathering her wits, she smiled at him. "Hi! Coming back from lunch, too?" she asked nervously.

"No, coming back from a client's," he replied in an amiable manner as he checked to make sure the button for the twentieth floor had been pushed. "Haven't eaten yet."

Now Nellie wished she hadn't gone out so early; if she'd waited, she might have managed to go out to lunch at the same time as he. *Find something clever to say,* she told herself, racking her brain. "Think it'll snow?" *Brilliant,* she chided herself sarcastically. No wonder she needed this book!

Kent nodded, unbuttoning his camel overcoat. "Looks like it—the sky's overcast. I love winter. When it snows, the city takes on a stately quality it doesn't have any other time of the year."

She drew her brows together. "Yes, I suppose snow looks more picturesque, but it sure messes up traffic and freezes the feet."

He grinned and his blue eyes flashed with humor as he glanced at her. "No doubt about it, you have to be tough to live in Chicago. Cold weather builds character. It's invigorating. Good for the soul."

"I...hadn't thought of it that way," she said, having difficulty finding anything to appreciate about dangerously slippery streets and sidewalks, high snowplow-created snowbanks to climb over or around, and toes gone stiff and numb from the cold, even inside fleece-lined boots.

The doors opened as the elevator arrived at the twentieth floor. Both got out. Nellie tried hard to think of something more to say, even about winter, but she drew a blank. Kent turned to go into his office and said, over his shoulder, "See you around."

"See you around," she repeated, feeling disappointed that yet again she'd let another little opportunity to connect with him slip by without making much progress. *Why was I born shy?* she asked herself impatiently. Neither of her parents, nor her famous older sister, had ever been shy. Why was she? Maybe that chapter on shyness would help.

She hung up her coat in the cloakroom and sat

down at the desk in her cubicle. It was separated from the cubicle next to it by a thin, five-foot-high partition. The desk on the other side had been given to a young male C.P.A. who had started with the firm when she had. His name was Rudy Jelinek, a hard-working, earnest fellow with light brown hair and a generous waistline. He'd often told her he'd be happy to have lunch with her anytime she was free. She wasn't sure if he was interested in her or just didn't like to eat by himself.

Rudy was out at a client's taking an inventory today, and the rest of the office seemed relatively empty. On the twentieth floor alone there were about twenty-five private offices, one of which was Kent's, and about fifty desks set apart in cubicles like hers, assigned to the staff accountants and the office secretaries and file clerks.

She hid the book in her bottom desk drawer, feeling rather sneaky, but hopeful. Getting back to work, she took out some spreadsheets from her small file cabinet. As she did, she was reminded of what had happened only yesterday and how devastated she'd felt. She'd been studying spreadsheets just as she was now, when Rudy had come in, returning from a client's office.

"Hi, Nellie," he'd said. "Heard the news?"

"What news?" she'd asked, looking up at him. He was peering over the partition between them.

"Kent Hastings is getting promoted to manager."

Nellie had gasped. "Really?"

"Not only that, but he's moving up to Worldwide on the thirty-fourth floor."

Nellie had shaken her head at first, thinking Rudy

must have been mistaken. Latham & Eliot's national headquarters occupied the eighteenth to the twenty-third floors of the building. The headquarters of the firm's international offices—they had branches in twelve foreign countries—was on the thirty-fourth and thirty-fifth floors. But she'd never heard of anyone, even at the manager level, being moved to the international office. And Kent had only just been promoted.

"Why would the firm transfer him up there?" she'd asked Rudy.

"I just heard the news on the way in. Don't know the details."

Someone must have gotten the details wrong, Nellie had assured herself. They just couldn't send Kent up to the thirty-fourth floor. If they did, how would she ever see him?

In about fifteen minutes, Arnie Hammersmith, a senior accountant and Kent's best friend, had come by carrying some files. He was tall, lanky and had red hair and a smattering of freckles. "Nellie, did you hear about Kent?"

"Rudy told me. Are they really sending him up to the thirty-fourth floor?"

"Yeah, it's true."

"Oh," she'd said, unable to disguise her disappointment. "Why?"

Arnie had looked as though he was trying to keep himself from smiling. He raised his red eyebrows. "Well, it seems Kent stood out from the crowd to the powers-that-be here," he'd told her in a gentle tone. "And he's worked with several clients over the years

that have overseas branches, so he's developed kind
of an expertise in that area.''

"I see," she'd said.

"By the way, I got promoted to manager, too."

Nellie had been so distressed, she hadn't processed
what Arnie had said for a few moments. When she
realized what he'd told her, she'd looked up and tried
to smile. "Oh, you did? Congratulations! You certainly deserve it."

"I'll be remaining here in the Manufacturing Division, though, so you'll still be seeing a lot of my
ugly puss," he'd joked.

"Good," she'd said absently. "I mean...you have
a nice face," she'd amended.

"So you won't mind seeing it?"

"Of course not."

"Um...how about lunch sometime?"

She'd looked up in surprise. "Sure, I'd be happy
to. Why? Will I be working with you again?" About
six months ago, she'd worked under his direction on
the audit of a paper manufacturer.

"Not that I know of. Hope so, though."

"Oh," she'd said, feeling confused.

"Free for lunch today?"

Nellie had felt her head swimming and didn't think
she'd be able to eat anything. "Thanks, but not today.
Some other time."

"I'll get back to you later then. We're doing lunch
soon, all right?"

She'd smiled. "I'll look forward to it."

After Arnie had walked away, Nellie had felt limp.
The thirty-fourth floor! Some days she didn't see Kent
even when he worked on this floor. She wouldn't be

running into him on the elevator anymore, either, because a different set of elevators serviced the top of the building. If she hadn't been able to get his attention by now, how would she ever win his notice if he worked so many floors up? It was hopeless. She'd felt so deflated, she could have wept. How long did she have left on the same floor with him?

When she'd seen Arnie coming out of the file room a little later, she'd waved him over. "I was just curious—when will Kent move to the thirty-fourth floor?"

"Two weeks," Arnie had said. "That's what he told me last night, anyway. We had dinner together to celebrate our promotions."

"Two weeks," she'd repeated, swallowing.

"That's all you wanted to ask me?" Arnie had said, an amused twinkle in his eye. "Nothing else on your mind but Kent?"

Arnie always seemed to enjoy hinting that he saw right through her, that he knew she adored Kent. She smiled with embarrassment. "Yes. Sorry I bothered you."

"Oh, it's no bother. Two weeks from now, maybe you'll begin to notice the other men on this floor."

After he'd left, she'd sat at her desk and stared unseeing at the work papers in front of her. Two weeks!

For so long, she'd felt convinced that Kent was perfect for her. When they'd worked together those few weeks she'd felt she'd finally met a man who seemed to be on the same wavelength as she. Like her, Kent was not athletically inclined, though he looked fit. He'd captured her heart one day at the candy factory when she'd mentioned her sister had won an Olympic gold medal for track. He'd joked that when he'd tried out for his college track team, he'd taken off down the field in the wrong direction. When he'd told her that, she suddenly had felt so at home with him—more so than with her own family.

He'd gone on to admit that the only sport he followed was baseball—a game that even she understood. He apparently was a die-hard Cubs fan, which she'd thought indicated a strong sense of loyalty on his part, since the Cubs rarely ever won. He and she were both good at business and math, more cerebrally than athletically blessed. They were so obviously well suited to each other, that a middle-aged woman who worked at the factory as a candy taster had whispered to Nellie that she and he looked perfect together. "As perfect as the bride and groom dolls on top of a wedding cake," she'd said.

Of course they were perfect for each other, Nellie thought as she arranged her work papers on her desk. Just because Kent didn't realize it, didn't mean that she should give up. Almost a year had gone by since the candy factory, and she hadn't been able to light his fire. What kind of fuel did it take? She wished she could call her sister, Jeannie, and get some advice, but she was busy in New York City shooting a TV commercial.

Get more competitive, Jeannie had once told her. But Nellie wasn't even sure who she was competing with. She hoped the advice in *How To Marry Your Dreamboat* would give her a decisive advantage over whatever women might currently be in Kent's life.

She had to make him see that she and she alone was the perfect mate for him.

That night at home after work, she opened the book. She only skimmed the first chapter, "When He Doesn't Know You Exist." The female author spent more time describing the condition and the reasons for it, which Nellie understood all too well from experience, than offering advice. The second chapter, however, "Shyness Can Be Sexy," gave Nellie hope. For example, it said that women who talked too much often got on men's nerves in the long run, and that many single men eventually discovered the calming, comforting company a quiet woman could offer them. Shy women were more often than not exceptionally attentive listeners, and men loved to have a woman listen to them talk.

The author also described how a woman could discover the mysterious power of silence. A quiet woman who kept a man wondering, *What is she thinking about?* held his interest, increased his adoration, perpetuated his yearning to get closer to her, in ways an able conversationalist, however witty, never could.

This method of luring men had become a lost art, the author declared. *Consider Greta Garbo,* she wrote. *For a woman of few words, the actress enchanted men for decades. Consider the cool and elusive Grace Kelly, the calm and radiant composure of Gene Tierney in* Laura *and the exquisite French actress, Catherine Deneuve, whose expressive eyes and face were far more memorable than her words. These were women who did not chatter, who chose their words carefully, whose eyes said volumes even when they weren't speaking. And they were admired by men of all ages on all continents.*

So, the author concluded, if a woman is not a whiz at making conversation, it didn't have to be a disadvantage. Indeed, with a bit of perception and a surer sense of oneself, the art of silence could become quite a valuable tool.

Nellie felt more confident the next morning as she walked to the office. If the book was right, perhaps she possessed a quality men actually would like, if she figured out how to use it correctly. As she walked through the revolving entrance doors of the building, she saw Kent up ahead, waiting by the elevator. She decided to put what she'd read last night to the test. Instead of working hard to keep up a conversation with him, she'd see if there really was any power in silence.

"Hello, Kent," she said as she came up beside him. "I don't think I've congratulated you yet on your promotion. I'm happy for you."

He turned to glance at her and smiled. "Thanks. You've heard already?"

"Good news travels fast," she said blithely. And then she said nothing more.

They both stood without speaking for a few moments, and then Kent glanced at her, as if wondering why she was so quiet. "Not as cold out today, is it?" he commented.

"No."

He rocked back on his heels a bit, looking up at the floor indicator above the elevator as if growing uncomfortable. "Here it is," he said as the doors opened. He allowed her to go in first, and he followed. No one else boarded, and the doors closed. He pressed the button marked twenty.

Nellie kept a serene smile on her face as she watched the floor numbers change above the door. Out of the corner of her eye, she could see Kent surreptitiously studying her.

"Well," he said, as if giving in to a pressure to break the silence, "guess I won't be going up this elevator much longer. I'll be on the thirty-fourth floor in a couple of weeks."

"I heard," she said, glancing at him. "Must be a nice view from up there."

"It is. My new office will be small, but you can see the lake and part of Grant Park from my window," he said with pride.

"Sounds spectacular," she commented as the doors opened. She stepped out and, looking back at him over her shoulder as she walked toward her desk, she said, "See you."

"See you," he muttered back, looking puzzled. She turned her head and continued her purposeful saunter to her cubicle. Inside she was smiling. *That went rather well,* she was thinking. Her change in demeanor from trying too hard to make a conversation to barely trying at all had drawn his attention and made him wonder. She remembered a favorite line of her sister's regarding her numerous boyfriends—"Always keep 'em guessing," Jeannie liked to say.

Nellie had finally figured out a way to do that.

# 2

Kent walked into his office in a distracted mood. He set his heavy briefcase on the floor, hung up his coat and paced. What was going on with Nellie? She'd heard he'd been promoted, and she didn't seem to care. He'd thought that she and his other co-workers might be a little sad about his move to the thirty-fourth floor. Indifference was a reaction he hadn't expected, and he felt rather deflated.

Not that he cared, really. But the last time they'd gone up in the elevator together, she'd made her usual effort to create conversation. Today, he might as well have been a cardboard cutout standing next to her. Just now when he'd gotten an enviable promotion and was moving to the top even faster than he'd hoped to, Nellie had suddenly burst his bubble with her polite, ho-hum attitude.

Kent blinked hard, impatient with himself. This was stupid. Why was he even thinking about Nellie? He had a date with a beautiful blonde at one in the afternoon.

He checked his watch. Damn, it was later than he'd thought. He grabbed his coat and hurried off to the Art Institute.

\* \* \*

That evening, Nellie continued to read her new book on the subway train to the Near North Side where her studio apartment was located. Once home, she heated up some soup for dinner. She was interrupted by a phone call from her sister, whom she hadn't heard from in several months.

"Hi, Nellie!" Jeannie always sounded happy, positive and confident. Nellie could picture her tossing back her lustrous brown hair as her green eyes sparkled with enthusiasm.

"Hi!" she responded in a lilting tone. "It's great to hear your voice. How's New York?"

"Beautiful. Wish you were here to see it with me. How are you? How's work?"

"Fine," Nellie replied, her tone growing half-hearted.

"Maybe I should have asked, how's Kent?"

"Don't ask," Nellie said with a groan.

Jeannie laughed. "Someday I've got to meet this guy. You never got so hooked on a man before."

"Because I was always in school trying to get good grades. I never had your flair for—"

"You have your own flair, Nellie. Just 'cause I got all the attention so far, doesn't mean that you won't shine on your own, too. I'm glad you've got your own apartment now. The best thing for you is to get away from Mom and Dad and stand on your own. I'm your biggest fan, you know that."

"I know. I've always been yours, too," Nellie said with affection. She was very proud of her big sister, an Olympics gold-medalist, sought after for talk shows, as a commentator for televised track-and-field events, and featured in several commercials and ads for athletic shoes, a soft drink and sportswear. The reason she'd flown to New York was to shoot a new commercial for the shoe company. "How did the shoot go?"

"Terrific. They wanted me to have a new hairstyle. It's still shoulder-length, but now it's layered instead of the blunt cut I used to have. It looks great, so I don't mind."

Nellie chuckled. "They're advertising shoes and they were worried about your *hair?*"

"Go figure. They shot scenes of me running in Central Park, and they thought my hair flew better cut this way."

The sisters laughed together for a moment.

"Seen Mom and Dad lately?" Jeannie asked.

"No. They keep wanting me to come for dinner, and I keep making excuses. My self-esteem is higher when I'm away from them."

"You mean, they still compare you to me?" Jeannie asked, sounding troubled. "Why? You graduated college with the highest honors. You passed that difficult C.P.A. exam on your first try."

"I know. I was amazed myself about passing the exam so fast. But you know Mom and Dad. Mom said, 'Oh, good.' Dad made one of his little jokes—'Too bad you weren't as good in sports as you are at pushing a pencil.'"

"Is that how they reacted when you told them?" Jeannie said with dismay. "I've been away too long. If I had been home, I would have set them straight! I should be there for you more than I am."

"No," Nellie objected. "I wouldn't want you to

curtail your career for me. You don't owe me anything. It's not your fault that you're the shining apple of their eye and I'm their 'other' daughter. You've always been very supportive and given me the affirmation I didn't get from them. Now I need to learn how to affirm myself. And I think I'm learning. So far, I'm doing well here at the firm. I'm confident I'll make senior accountant in a couple of years.''

"You'll make partner!''

Nellie smiled. "Well, that'll take a while," she explained. Jeannie didn't know much about the internal structure of a major accounting firm. "After senior accountant, I have to make manager and then partner. It's a tough ladder to climb. And I hope they don't have a glass ceiling for women. There is one woman partner now, so I'm hopeful there won't be any problem that way. I need to get more competitive though as you've always told me. It's not natural for me, the_ way it is for you. That's one reason I was never good in sports. That and lack of coordination." She chuckled. "And two left feet."

"Life isn't fair. I got the coordination, and you got all the brains!''

"You got all the boyfriends, too," Nellie reminded her.

"Your day will come. Becoming more competitive will probably help out in that department, too."

"But how?"

"What about your adorable Kent? Does he have a girlfriend?"

"Not a steady one, as far as I can find out. But he dates a lot. He often has lunch hour dates, when he takes a woman to the Art Institute. I happened to see him there once with a blonde at lunchtime. I mentioned it to Arnie, his buddy here, and Arnie said he takes women there all the time. The Impressionists are his favorites, I think. That's where I saw him that day, in a hall displaying Renoirs and Monets.''

''The Art Institute? Must be a classy guy.''

''*I* think so. Of course, he never took me there, when we worked together at the candy factory.'' Nellie sighed. ''The factory was on the West side, though—too far away. But back to what we were talking about—how does getting competitive help?''

''You've got to drum up a more ruthless attitude toward the women that he *does* take there. Figure out how to get a step up on your competition.''

''How?''

''Well, bone up on the Impressionists and start talking to him about those artists.''

Nellie drew her brows together. ''You think that would work?''

''It can't hurt. It would give you an edge over women he meets who know nothing about art.''

''I see. Well, he seems to like blondes. Do I have to bleach my brown hair to be competitive?'' Nellie asked, tongue in cheek.

''No way! Just be your beautiful self. And don't hide your light under a bushel.''

''Okay,'' Nellie said with a rueful chuckle. ''Thanks for the pep talk. When do you leave for France?'' She knew Jeannie was scheduled to be a participant on a planning committee for future Olympiads.

''Tomorrow morning. I'll be staying there for a while on sort of a vacation. I need one. Besides, I've got a new man in my life, and he wants to spend some time there with me.''

''Who?'' Nellie asked, all ears.

''He's another well-known athlete. I'd rather not say who just yet, but he just might turn out to be Mr. Right.''

Nellie felt surprisingly deflated. ''Now you'll go off and get married, and then I'll *never* see you.''

''Of course, you'll see me. Besides, you'll be so busy courting your own man that you won't even think about me.''

''Right,'' Nellie said, wishing it could be true. ''Well, have a great time in France. Call me when you can.''

Jeannie promised to phone when she returned to the U.S. and said goodbye. As Nellie replaced the phone receiver, she grew wistful. Jeannie had always made her feel taller than her five-foot-three stature. She was the perfect older sister, almost a second mom—and a better mom than the one they had. But Jeannie had her own life, and so now did Nellie.

Finishing her soup, Nellie reflected on her sister's advice, then went on reading. One of the chapters advised the reader to find out what her dreamboat's interests were and to develop an enthusiasm for those interests herself. This reminded Nellie of what her sister had said about boning up on the Impressionists. The book went on to describe how acquiring a genuine interest in the activities or hobbies a man enjoyed was a way of getting closer to him, even becoming a part of his life by participating in those activities with him.

The problem was, Nellie only had two weeks, so

it would be difficult to acquire a genuine interest in the things Kent enjoyed. She didn't even know what they all were yet. In her case, she only had time to ferret out his secret pleasures and learn enough about them to *pretend* a knowledge and interest in them herself.

Before going to sleep that night, Nellie sat up in bed with a pad and pencil, making a list of the things she already knew Kent liked:

1. Winter
2. Baseball, especially the Cubs
3. Art Institute, especially the Impressionists
4. Monopoly—hates checkers

What a short list, she thought, looking at it with dismay. This was all she'd been able to come up with. The last point she remembered from when she'd worked with him at the candy factory. They were talking about presents they'd each gotten from their families at Christmas. Someone had given him an onyx combination checkers and chess set. He'd said the carved stone was beautiful, but he'd only be able to use it for display. He never played chess much, he'd told her, and complained that he absolutely hated checkers. When she'd asked what game he did like, he'd replied, "Monopoly. Loved it ever since I was a kid."

Nellie shook her head, wondering how she could have been acquainted with someone for almost a year and still know so little about him. She'd have to find a way to learn more and make this list longer. How?

Arnie, she thought. Maybe when she went out to

lunch with him, she could pump him for some information about Kent. But that certainly wasn't being very fair to Arnie, her conscience told her. On the other hand, he already seemed to know that she admired Kent, so asking about Kent's likes and dislikes wouldn't surprise him. He'd shown patience with her, even if he was hoping she'd get over his friend. Perhaps Arnie would continue to be patient.

Nellie sighed fretfully and chewed her pencil. She hated taking advantage of Arnie, but what else could she do? She was short of time and growing desperate. And all was fair in love and war, right?

The next day Arnie had already arranged a lunch date with a client, so she had to put it off until the following day. She didn't wait to see if Arnie would ask her again; instead she walked into his office and invited him to lunch. "I'll treat. I'm afraid I have an ulterior motive," she confessed, having decided honesty was the best policy.

Arnie narrowed his eyes and smiled. "You, an ulterior motive? Now you've got me curious. Okay, I'm always happy to have a lady take me out."

She took him to a well-known restaurant at the Palmer House, one of Chicago's historic hotels. After they were seated at a table and had ordered, Arnie looked around at the opulent decor. "You've got nice taste," he said.

"Thanks." It wasn't so much her good taste, but she'd wanted to take him somewhere special to make up for her reason for buying him lunch. "So," she said, swallowing her pride, "about my ulterior motive."

Arnie studied her, full of attention. "Tell me."

She lowered her eyes to the tablecloth. "You probably won't be all that surprised. I'd like you to talk about Kent."

"Kent?" Arnie's expression fell. But after a moment, he smiled in a resigned way. "What do you want to know about him?"

"What his interests are, his likes and dislikes, his hobbies, his…raison d'être."

Arnie arched one eyebrow. "His reason for living? That's simple—to get ahead, climb the ladder of success to the top. Look up ambition in the dictionary and you'll see Kent's picture there."

Nellie's shoulders sank a bit. "Really? I knew he was aiming high, but I didn't realize—"

"Success is all he thinks about. He's very competitive."

"Oh." Now Nellie really felt deflated. In her personal life experience, competitive was not an uplifting word.

"Why do you want to know all about Kent?" Arnie asked.

"Because…look, I'll be straight with you. It would be silly of me to invent excuses for asking you for information. The fact is, he's leaving for the thirty-fourth floor, and once he does, my hopes to ever win his attention are dashed. I thought if I knew more about him, I'd be better able to talk about things that might interest him, and that way there still may be a chance I can get him interested in me. Sorry if I sound like a gushy schoolgirl, but I really, really like him, and this is my last chance." She searched Arnie's eyes for some sign of understanding from him.

He gave her a slight look of sympathy. "Kent's a mover and a shaker. It's no surprise he was chosen to move up to Worldwide. Feelings and emotions get in his way. You'd do better with someone more quiet and steady, like you are."

"I know that's probably sensible advice. But love isn't always sensible."

"Love?" Arnie let out a long exhale and slowly nodded his head. "Okay. Then this is probably not a bad idea. You use any ammunition you can muster, make one last attempt to ambush him and get his attention. If you get lucky, it works. If it doesn't, then when he goes bye-bye to the thirty-fourth floor, you'll know you did all you could to snare him and failed. Maybe then you'll be able to move on to greener, more productive pastures."

"Yeah," Nellie said with a sigh. "That probably sums up where I'm at. So…you'll help me?"

"Sure." He shifted his water glass to one side. "Let's see. His hobbies…did you know he once played the saxophone?"

"The saxophone?" she said with astonishment, opening her purse to get out her pad and pencil to add to her list.

"In high school. He played in the band. He told me that just the other day."

"So what kind of music does he like?" she asked, her pencil poised.

"Jazz. Gershwin. *Porgy and Bess.* Oh, and ragtime. He likes that old piano player—Scott Joplin. You know, the music from *The Sting.*"

As Nellie scribbled notes, questions poured into her

mind. "Great. What about food? Cajun? Oriental? Italian?"

"Loves Italian. And red wine. Merlot. Always orders cannoli for dessert. He's part Scandinavian, so he also likes things like pickled herring. It's his family's tradition to have that with meals, you know, like some people put olives and pickles out on the table? But he also eats it as a snack." Arnie laughed. "I remember I was up at his place once watching baseball on TV, and that's what he offered me. No popcorn, no pretzels. Beer and pickled herring. I couldn't stop laughing."

Nellie chuckled. "He told me a long time ago that he lives in an apartment off of Lake Shore Drive. Is he still there?"

"Yeah. Cedar Street."

"Cedar? That's not far from where I live," Nellie said, her eyes widening. "Gosh, where does he shop for groceries?"

Arnie lifted his shoulders. "Like I would know? Guys don't shoot the breeze about stuff like that."

"Right. Well, tell me more," she said, pencil ready, feeling primed. This was going better than she'd imagined it could. Why hadn't she bought that book sooner, or thought of this herself? Armed with all this new knowledge, she had to succeed.

When lunch was over, Nellie had half a dozen scratch pad pages of notes. She happily accepted the bill the waiter brought and gave him her credit card.

"Thanks for lunch," Arnie said, looking satisfied.

"You're welcome! Thanks for all the information. Now, you won't snitch on me, will you? I know you and Kent are friends, but I was hoping that this could remain our little secret.''

Arnie extended his hand across the table to shake her hand in agreement. ''Our little secret,'' he said, giving her fingers an extra squeeze. ''I just have one request.''

''Sure,'' she said, withdrawing her hand. ''What?''

''If and when your strategy to lasso Kent fails, then would you try it out on me next? I'll be happy to tell you all my idiosyncrasies and you can use the info on me any way you like. I can guarantee you'll get better results.''

Nellie smiled warmly at him. Arnie had such a pleasant disposition and a good sense of humor. Though he was always carefree and joking around her, she'd sometimes sensed he might be attracted to her. Too bad she hadn't fallen in love with him. He'd make some woman a nice husband. ''I'll remember that. Thanks, Arnie.''

They went back to the office. When they came out of the elevator on the twentieth floor, Kent happened to be talking to someone in Personnel nearby. He looked surprised to see them returning from lunch together. But he was involved in his conversation and unable to speak to either of them.

Fine, Nellie thought. Let Kent think whatever he wants. If her scheme worked, he'd soon be seeing her in a new and different light.

On the other hand, she might be on her way to making a major fool of herself. But she had to try to climb this precarious ladder she was building rung by rung to successfully win his heart. If she fell flat on her face, well, at least she'd given it her best shot.

* * *

The next day at noon, Kent grabbed his overcoat from his desk, where he'd tossed it a few minutes ago. He'd stopped back at his office after returning from his client's to drop off his heavy briefcase and to pick up Arnie for lunch. He walked across the floor to Arnie's office and found him working at his computer.

"I'm back. Ready to eat?" Kent asked, putting on the overcoat again. They'd agreed yesterday afternoon to meet today for lunch.

Arnie looked up. "Yeah, I'm starving. Get stuck at the client's?"

"Some questions on the billing. Got it squared away. Let's go."

They took a cab to Berghoff's, an old German restaurant on Adams Street, Arnie's favorite place to eat. Arnie ordered sauerbraten and Kent ordered Wiener schnitzel. When the white-aproned waiter took their menus and left, Kent leaned back in his chair, enjoying the restaurant's masculine atmosphere with its carved woodwork and rich oak paneling.

Arnie, usually talkative, had been quiet in the cab and now was saying little, as if something was bothering him.

"What's on your mind?" Kent asked. He and Arnie had always been direct with each other—it was something that Kent had liked about their rapport ever since they'd started together at the firm. Over the five years since, they'd developed a solid friendship.

"What do you think of Nellie?" Arnie asked, looking him in the eye. "You try to treat her the same as everyone else, but you don't. Why?"

"I don't?"

"No. You're always a little reserved around her. You hurt her feelings."

Kent was baffled. "I don't think I hurt her feelings."

"You never bother to look at her long enough to notice the disappointment in her eyes," Arnie said.

Kent smiled. "I think you're the one who has an issue with her—I think you're attracted to her. You had lunch with her yesterday, didn't you?"

"Yes," Arnie said a bit defensively. "I think she's a nice person. She's sweet and caring. And she *is* attractive—maybe not in a flashy way, but she has an inner beauty."

Kent shrugged his shoulders. "If you're so impressed, go after her."

"I would, if I thought there was any hope. She's so hung up on you, she doesn't notice the rest of us. I think Rudy likes her, too. But she only has eyes for you."

"Me?" Kent replied, feeling uncomfortable with the sudden flicker of awareness he felt. "You don't know if that's true. Did she *say* that?"

"I don't get it," Arnie persisted. "You claim you're ready to get married, and yet you pass up a girl who'd make a beautiful wife and she's already in love with you."

"In *love?* With *me?* Why would she be? Are you making this up?"

"It's been obvious to almost everyone on the floor for nearly a year now."

Totally astonished, Kent collapsed against the back of his wood chair. Why would Nellie have become so attached to him? He couldn't believe it. He'd done nothing to lead her on. Arnie must be misinformed or imagining things.

Kent leaned forward, setting his elbows on the table. "Whether what you say is true or not," he stated, reluctant to question Arnie's convictions, "she's not what I'm looking for." He grew a little defensive, though he didn't know why. "Nothing against her. To me, she's sort of like a kid sister, or a cousin. I appreciate her hard work and intelligence. And she's sweet. But in my eyes, she's not someone to date."

"You like blondes," Arnie surmised, apparently recalling the various women he'd seen with Kent over the years.

"A redhead might do." Kent unfolded his napkin and slipped it onto his lap, prepared to enlighten his friend with his personal theory if Arnie continued in this vein.

"A redhead might *do?*" Arnie repeated, looking puzzled. "What does that mean? You have a list of qualifications a woman's got to have for you to date her?"

Kent paused. The way Arnie put it, it sounded a little cold. "I…hadn't thought of it as a list exactly. But I have figured out what I want in a wife."

"You have?"

"Sure. Setting goals, following a plan—that's how you get ahead."

"So a wife is like a goal to you?"

Again, Kent felt annoyed at the rigid interpretation Arnie seemed to put on Kent's plans. "Look, why are we at Latham & Eliot? What do we both want?"

"Make partner."

"Right. I'd like to make partner by the time I'm thirty-five."

Arnie raised his eyebrows. "God, that's pushing it."

"Being ambitious never hurt anyone—it makes people notice. I'm twenty-nine now. I've got six years to accomplish that goal. And, as we all know, being married is considered an asset in the business world—people always wonder about a guy who's still single once he gets to be about thirty. So, we both need to be on the lookout for a wife. Right?"

"Right."

Kent picked up his fork, pointing it in the air for emphasis. "Now, let's consider the partners the firm has at the moment. Take the partners in our division specifically. Ever notice what their wives are like?"

Arnie scratched his ear. "We don't see the spouses that often—just at the Christmas party and the July picnic."

"That's true. But at the Christmas party last month, I made a little study. Of the nineteen wives, twelve of them were blondes and two were redheads. The other five were brown-haired or gray-haired. And most of the women had some pizzazz in the way they dressed, and most of them were also outgoing and talkative."

"Sounds like you made a regular inventory of them."

"I did. And my conclusion—something I'd already suspected, anyway—was that to make partner, having the right wife can be a real asset."

"And the 'right' wife is a blond social butterfly?"

Again, Kent felt accused of being coldly analytical.

"Well, that's boiling it down a lot. Of course, there's room for variation."

"What about—you know—falling in love and all that jazz?"

"Women have a saying that it's as easy to fall in love with a rich man as a poor man. All I'm saying is, it's as easy for me to fall for a vivacious blonde as a shy brunette."

"Aha," Arnie said quietly. "And Nellie is the shy brunette."

Kent felt taken aback. "I didn't say—"

Arnie pointed his finger at Kent. "I thought, early on when you worked with her, that there were vibes going on between you and her," Arnie said, his eyes alight. "Now I understand why you didn't pursue her. You ruled her out because she didn't qualify according to your list of perfect wife traits."

Kent put down his fork, set his elbow on the table and rubbed his forehead. "Vibes? Maybe there was a brief...a sort of passing attraction between us, but it didn't go anywhere. She *is* shy, the quintessential girl next door. Not my type. I doubt that I'm her type, either, if she stopped to think about it." Kent noticed Arnie look down at the tabletop. "She *will* make someone a nice wife. Not me, though."

"Okay," Arnie said, looking up with a smug grin. "Now that I know that for sure, I think I *will* go after her myself."

Kent stared at his friend. He felt a sudden, inexplicable flare of hostility toward Arnie.

Arnie was studying Kent's eyes. "That sure got your dander up! You can't have it both ways. If you're going to pass her by, then one of these days she's bound to get over you and accept some other guy into her life. It might as well be me."

Kent quelled his perplexing ill humor. "Sure. Go after her. I'm not in your way."

"Thanks!"

Kent tried to make light of their conversation. "You mean, after the benefit of all my research and advice for making partner, you're not going to look for a blonde, too?"

"I guess I must not be quite as ambitious as you. I want a nice comfy home life with a woman who really suits me, and I don't care what color her hair is. If that means I'll never make partner, well, that's okay. I can always start my own little C.P.A. firm and be happy. I don't believe in success at any price. That, to me, isn't true success."

Kent nodded with respect. "Okay. Maybe we have slightly different philosophies."

"My dad was a bus driver," Arnie continued. "I had to put myself through college. We didn't have much, but we had a nice home life, my dad, my mom, and my brother and me. That's what I want most."

Kent felt he understood. "My dad worked at a bank. He was a branch manager, but he never was able to climb any higher on the corporate ladder. He made an adequate living and provided some help putting me through college. Fortunately for his financial situation, I was an only child. But we had a nice home life—I know what you mean about that."

"What's your mom like?" Arnie asked, looking curious. "Did your dad marry the type of woman you're looking for?"

Kent smiled and bowed his head. "No. My mom

is the old-fashioned sort who stayed home to raise me. She's a quiet homebody and she gets nervous and shy at social events.''

''You think that had anything to do with your dad's not climbing the success ladder?''

''Well, she's the salt of the earth, but in that particular regard, no, she wasn't an asset to him. She's beautiful, honest, loyal and sweet. I suspect my dad fell for her pretty hard when he met her. He married with his heart, you see, not with his head. I plan to use my head *and* my heart to find the right wife.''

The waiter brought their food, and Kent was glad for the distraction. He hadn't meant to get on a soapbox, and he hoped he hadn't offended Arnie.

They changed the subject and the rest of their lunch was much more relaxed.

When Kent returned to the office, he almost bumped into Nellie, who was coming from the file room and carrying some large, thick folders crammed full of work papers. He helped steady the folders, for she'd almost dropped them. ''Sorry,'' he said. ''Okay now?''

She looked up at him, her brown eyes shining. ''Yes, thanks.''

Kent remembered that glow in her eyes from ten months ago on the job together at the candy factory. She'd always made him feel strong the way she looked up at him. He also remembered the unexpected flashes of humor and whimsy in her large brown eyes, surprising in a woman who was basically shy. Most women of his acquaintance played coy games and knew when and how to flirt and when to play it cool. There was none of that with Nellie. She was a capable businesswoman, yet when it came to personal relationships, she seemed so vulnerable. That vulnerability was strangely appealing and had unexpectedly tugged at his heart. He'd almost been tempted to get to know her better, explore what she was all about.

But soon he'd realized that she was a lot like his mom in her quiet sincerity. His dad had gone soft on a woman who didn't suit his career, and Kent wasn't going to allow himself to go soft on a woman like Nellie. Since she'd reminded him of his mom, Kent had purposely begun to look at her as he would one of his relatives—like a sister or cousin, as he'd told Arnie. The habit of seeing her in that light seemed natural to him now, and he'd convinced himself that the special warmth he always saw in Nellie's eyes wasn't meant for him in particular. She just had lovely eyes, that's all.

"Heard you did a good job on the McClellan audit," he said, maintaining a businesslike manner. "Keep up the good work."

She lowered her gaze. "I will," she said, then walked on by him.

Well, Kent thought, heading into his private office, guess she's still in her indifferent mode. Apparently she didn't give a damn that he was moving to the thirty-fourth floor. And Arnie thought she had a crush on him! People imagined the craziest things. Thank God she didn't. A girl like her just didn't fit into his life plan.

Kent sat behind his desk and took out a client's work papers, arranging them in front of him in an organized way. Got to have a plan, he told himself, feeling edgy and irritable now. Got to have a plan, or you won't get what you want. And Kent knew what he wanted—in fact, with his promotion, he was well on his way to having it all. He was absolutely sure of himself, no doubts, no questions, no reservations. It was good to be sure, and he was. So he ought to be happy.

Well, he *was* happy, damn it! These inexplicable moods would come and then go—no use taking them seriously. Little yens for what might have been shouldn't be indulged. He was happy on his chosen path. And once he found the right woman, he'd be even happier.

## 3

Nellie spent an entire evening creating a work sheet on yellow columnar paper. She felt the need to organize her project in some way, much as she did her audits, so that she could evaluate her progress as she went along. An accountant's columnar pad was the tool she was used to using.

In the wide column on the left, she listed all the things she'd learned that Kent liked. In the next column she noted where she'd gotten the information—Arnie's name was written in often here. The third column would be reserved to record the date and place on which she'd used that particular topic in conversation, either with Kent or within his earshot. In the next column she would note Kent's reaction to the conversation, that is, whether he seemed to take notice, whether he appeared interested or disinterested. In the final column she would rate herself on her effectiveness on a scale of one to ten.

Using decorative magnets, she posted the ten by fourteen work sheet on her refrigerator. Now she felt organized and mentally set. All she had to do was put her plan into action.

* * *

The next morning at the office, Nellie seized her first opportunity. Having arrived early, she saw Kent and Arnie coming off the elevator together. Both were unbuttoning their heavy wool overcoats, wet with droplets from melting snow. Picking up a file on her desk that needed to be returned to the file room, she chose a path that put herself in their way.

"'Morning, Arnie. Hi, Kent," she said in a breezy manner. "Frosty enough for you? This cold front is really invigorating. And last night when the temperature dipped, I couldn't help but notice how beautiful sleet looks when it freezes on trees."

Arnie turned his head away, looking across the room as he stifled a laugh. Kent, however, paused to stare at her for a moment.

"You're right," Kent said somewhat archly as he brushed droplets off his coat. "I noticed that as I was getting white stains on my new shoes from the salt they'd sprinkled on the icy sidewalk in front of my building."

Nellie was surprised at his sardonic response. "I've heard vinegar gets salt stains off of leather."

"Really? I'll try it." He hesitated, as if mentally correcting his attitude. He smiled and added in a more positive tone, "It did look sort of magical with the ice frozen on all the little tree branches."

"I thought so," she replied with a grin. And then, reminding herself not to look as if she was trying too hard to make conversation, she purposefully moved on toward the file room. She felt her predesigned encounter with him had gone pretty well.

Her next opportunity came that afternoon. She ran

into Kent on purpose once again when she saw him walk over to the coffee machine.

"Hi," Kent said, looking up in surprise as he poured powdered cream into his coffee. They'd never run into each other at the coffeemaker before. The reason was that Nellie didn't drink coffee. She actually preferred cold drinks.

"Hi," she replied, pouring herself some hot water. "Thought I'd try some tea." As he stirred his coffee and she found a tea bag in a box by the machine, she asked, "Do you happen to know of a music store that has a good selection of jazz tapes and CDs?"

Kent's eyes brightened. "Sure. There's one near Wabash and Madison. You like jazz?"

"I'm not that familiar with it, actually. But I was listening to the radio last night, and I heard one piece that featured the saxophone that I really liked. I didn't catch the name of it, but I thought I'd browse around and see what I could find."

He smiled, his blue eyes searching hers. "You like the sax? I used to play it, in high school."

"Did you? I've always thought it had an evocative sound that sort of gets under your skin," Nellie said, improvising. She barely could recognize one wind instrument from another.

"I agree. It's popular for its fluid, sexy sound."

Nellie swallowed. She'd never heard the word sexy come out of Kent's mouth before. "Right. I…was also hoping to find some ragtime recordings. Scott Joplin perhaps."

"Sure, the store on Madison has that, too. You like Joplin?"

"Well, I happened to see *The Sting* on TV recently, and I enjoyed the piano playing in the background," she told him, though actually she'd rented the tape. "I'm trying to broaden my knowledge of music. I never played an instrument when I was growing up. My family was totally sports oriented."

"You're starting in a good way," Kent complimented her. "Most people would try to learn about classical music first, and then might lose interest because it's too highbrow. Jazz—which grew out of ragtime, by the way—is uniquely American. Easy to listen to. That's what I like about it."

She smiled at him, almost flirtatiously, as she'd seen her sister do years ago with her high school boyfriends. Her heart was pounding faster than Jeannie's probably ever had, however. "I feel like I've just had my first music lesson. Thank you."

He blinked and glanced down. "Welcome." He seemed a bit thrown or perhaps confused. "I'd better get back to work."

As he walked away toward his office, Nellie inhaled deeply, feeling slightly light-headed. That was the longest conversation she'd had with Kent since she'd worked with him at the candy factory. He'd actually seemed interested in talking to her and wasn't anxious to be on his way—that is, until she'd tried her sister's tactics.

Perhaps she shouldn't have imitated Jeannie's method of entrancing men. Far from attracting Kent, she may have scared him away. She needed to fine-tune herself, so as not to look shy, but not to come on so strong that she seemed artificial.

God, this was hard work. But if she could win Kent, it would be worth every drop of sweat she put into it.

Something seemed to be a little offbeat about Nellie today, Kent thought to himself as he sat down at his desk. She certainly had lost her indifference—in fact, she had more to say than usual. And she seemed to have also lost her shyness. He wondered what was going on with her. And the way she'd looked at him a few minutes ago—what was he supposed to make of that? Was Arnie right? Did Nellie have a crush on him?

Later, as he was leaving for the day, he somehow wasn't surprised when she happened to walk up to the elevator just after he'd pressed the button marked Down. He smiled, but said nothing. He'd responded to her a little too enthusiastically by the coffee machine.

Kent expected her to say she was on her way to Wabash and Madison to look at jazz tapes. But she surprised him again when she asked, "You like Monopoly, don't you?"

"It's my favorite game," he replied as the doors opened. The elevator was almost full, but they squeezed in.

"I thought you mentioned that a long time ago. I'm collecting them."

"Collecting them?" he repeated, puzzled, as the doors closed and the elevator swooshed downward.

"I have a British version and a French version," she said, "based on London and Paris. The Chicago version, too. I also have one for the University of Illinois campus, where I went to school. And I have the standard version, of course. That's my collection, so far. I'd like to find a vintage copy, though. You know, one from decades ago when the game first came out. I think that would be a nice addition.''

The doors opened and Kent and Nellie stepped out into the first-floor lobby. Kent's mind boggled. He'd thought he was a Monopoly fan, but it had never occurred to him to collect the various versions of the game. ''Amazing,'' he said.

''You wouldn't happen to know where I could get an antique copy?'' she asked.

''No idea.''

''I'll check with some antiques dealers. 'Night,'' she said blithely and walked off, mixing in with the others moving through the lobby toward the swiveling exit doors.

'''Night.'' Kent was a little surprised that she didn't stay alongside of him and try to keep their conversation going. Obviously she *wasn't* chasing him, or she would have. But it was odd—why did she strike up a conversation about Monopoly, of all things?

Well, she'd said she remembered that he liked the game. Perhaps he'd also once mentioned that he liked jazz, and that was why she'd asked him about music stores that afternoon. Apparently she'd viewed him today as a possible source of information about subjects she was currently exploring.

Hmm. She liked a lot of the same things he liked. As he walked out of the building and onto the snowy street, he imagined himself spending a pleasant Sunday afternoon with her playing Monopoly and listening to jazz tapes.

No, he told himself, dispersing his comfortable mental image. So she's interested in ragtime and likes to collect Get Out Of Jail Free cards. For those two minor things in common, there were many more ways in which he and she were mismatched. *Stick to your plan, reach your goal,* he reminded himself.

But that night, he suddenly awoke from a surprisingly erotic dream that left him breathless, heart pounding and as hot as a rod just pulled from the fire. He'd dreamed he was in bed with a woman, deep in the throes of sensual passion. The content of the dream didn't alarm him. It was the woman he'd dreamed he was with—Nellie.

*Forget it,* he quickly told himself. *It doesn't mean a thing.* He tossed and turned most of the night and by morning he'd convinced himself that dreams had nothing to do with real life, no matter what the damned psychologists might say.

Early that Friday evening, at home after work, Nellie took down the yellow columnar sheet off her refrigerator, sat down at her small kitchen table and noted the topic she'd managed to raise today in Kent's earshot. She'd asked Arnie, while Kent happened to be passing by, if he believed the so-called billy goat curse was the reason that the Cubs hadn't played in a World Series since 1945.

She'd learned about the story in a conversation yesterday with the middle-aged security man at the front desk in her apartment building, whom she knew was a loyal Cubs fan. He'd told her about the local folklore regarding a man who'd tried to bring his pet billy goat to the Cubs' World Series game. He was not allowed to bring the animal into Wrigley Field and, because of this, the story went, the outraged man cursed the Cubs, saying they would never play in a World Series again.

When she'd asked Arnie about the curse, Kent had paused, drawn into the conversation.

"Nah, that's just a story," Arnie had said. "I don't believe in curses."

"Whether it happened or not," Kent had interjected, "the story could have a subliminal effect. Players are often superstitious."

Arnie had laughed. "That's the lamest excuse I've heard for the Cubs' half-century losing streak. They just never get their act together, that's all."

Many Chicagoans, at an early age, chose one home team or the other to rally behind for life. Arnie, it had become clear, was a White Sox fan.

Nellie had seen the indignant sparks in Kent's eyes and she'd jumped on the opportunity to side with him. "No, I think he's right," she'd told Arnie. "My sister always ran with her lucky gold chain around her neck. Once she panicked before a meet because she couldn't find it. Fortunately she located it at the last minute and won. It may be all in their heads, but superstition is a powerful thing for sports people."

"Right!" Kent had agreed, standing closer to Nellie as they both had faced down Arnie.

"Yeah, but to be cowed by a superstition for fifty years?" Arnie had retorted with amusement. "I'd say to the Cubs, 'Get over it!'" With that parting shot, he'd walked away.

Kent had chuckled and turned to Nellie. "I didn't

know you were a Cubs fan,'' he'd said, apparently assuming she must be one.

Nellie frankly didn't feel one way or another about either team, but she'd smiled and said, ''I suppose I like to root for the underdog.''

''Ever been to a game?'' he'd asked.

''When I was a kid.''

''You should go again. Even with the modern lighting, Wrigley Field still has that old-time magic.'' He'd hesitated then. She'd had the feeling he might be toying with the idea of asking her to go to a game with him. But spring was a few months off, and he'd said nothing more on the subject, except, ''Thanks for seconding my argument with Arnie.''

As she sat at her kitchen table now and thought over the incident while recording it on her columnar sheet, she decided that this was her most successful attempt to get Kent's attention so far. When she came to the column in which she rated her effectiveness, she rewarded herself with a score of eight, her best yet.

She reviewed the sheet and decided she certainly was a lot further along than she had been several days ago when she began her campaign. Kent was noticing her more often and in a more positive way than he had in a long, long while. But she still had a long way to go, and not much time. She wanted to find a way to meet him outside the office, if she could, away from their normal work situation, so he could see her in a different atmosphere.

Chewing on her pencil, she recalled that Arnie had said Kent lived on Cedar Street, not far from her apartment, but Arnie didn't know where he grocery shopped. Nellie got out the yellow pages and looked up grocery stores, checking the ones in the neighborhood. She was familiar with two, both of which she'd shopped at herself, but there was a third, she noted, closer to Kent's apartment that she hadn't known about.

She also remembered Arnie had said Kent liked pickled herring. That might help to narrow the choices. She got on the phone and called the two she was familiar with, asking if they carried pickled herring. Since she'd never wanted to buy the item, she had no idea if the stores stocked it.

Neither store sold pickled herring. She called the third store, the one she'd never been to. A man answered.

"Gable's Grocery and Deli. We closed at seven."

"Oh, sorry." Nellie glanced at her kitchen wall clock. It showed five after seven. "I was just wondering if you have pickled herring."

"Sure. By the pound in the deli section. Come by tomorrow."

"Okay. What are your hours?"

"Eight to five on Saturday. Closed Sunday."

He sounded anxious to end the call, but Nellie persisted. "A co-worker of mine likes pickled herring. I wondered if he bought it at your store. Kent Hastings?"

"Kent? Sure. He's in here every Saturday."

She wanted to ask what time he usually showed up, but embarrassment got to her. And she didn't want the store clerk telling Kent about the phone call. "Then you must have the best pickled herring in town. I know he's particular. I'll stop by. Thanks."

Nellie felt slightly short of breath as she hung up. She wasn't used to stratagems and subterfuge to glean information from strangers. At least with Arnie she'd been able to be honest. She'd felt like a spy calling the grocery store.

But she'd found out what she'd wanted to learn, so she quickly got over her embarrassment about her method. Now she knew it was very likely Kent would stop by Gable's Grocery tomorrow, sometime between eight and five. As she went to the refrigerator to get a cold drink, a memory popped into her mind. When they were at the candy factory, she recalled Kent telling her that he liked to sleep late on Saturdays. So she probably didn't need to start staking out the store at eight in the morning. But, to be safe, she probably ought to be there by ten.

Nellie spent the rest of the evening deciding what to wear. She pulled out a sweater her sister had sent her for Christmas. So far, she hadn't had nerve enough to wear it anywhere. Time to get over her inhibitions, she told herself, as she tried it on in front of a mirror. Besides, the color suited her and gave her a certain glow.

Or perhaps she was just blushing at herself.

The next morning, Nellie drove the half mile to Gable's Grocery. It was a corner store, rather old-fashioned in its plain, cramped, no-frills appearance. She found a parking spot across the street and a few doors down, where, even sitting low behind her steering wheel, her hair stuffed under a Cubs baseball cap with the brim over her eyes, she could see who came and left the store. Again, she grew embarrassed at the lengths to which she was going to chase Kent. She almost felt like some tacky private detective. She hoped that someday, when—and if—she was married to Kent, she'd be able to laugh about her tactics. One thing was certain, however—she'd never *tell* him about them.

It was a sunny day, and warmer than it had been during the week. Despite the improved weather, after an hour, Nellie was beginning to feel stiff and cold from sitting in the same position for so long. One foot had fallen asleep, and she shook it and squirmed to get the circulation back.

All at once, she forgot about the pins and needles in her toes. A tall, dark-haired young man had just come around the corner. It was definitely Kent. She recognized his coat and the long strides he took. Her heart began to pound. *My God, my plan is working!* she thought. She waited a minute to compose herself, then got out of her car and headed for the store.

Kent was taking a box of cereal off the grocery shelf when suddenly he heard his name.

"Kent! For heaven's sake. Do you shop here?"

He turned around and found Nellie looking up at him, her brown eyes warm and radiant. Her long hair, usually pulled back with barrettes, flowed loose and thick around her shoulders. Her winter jacket was unbuttoned. Underneath he saw her vivid apricot-colored sweater and the ample glimpse of cleavage its deep V neckline revealed. She had on jeans, but Kent was too distracted by the curves under her sweater to pay much attention to the lower part of her body. Nellie looked completely different from the way she appeared at work in her boxy, buttoned up gray suits. She looked even better than she had in his dream. *Forget the dream!* he reprimanded himself, wary of his own straying thoughts.

"Yeah, I shop here," he said. He didn't realize his grip on the cereal box had loosened. As it began to slip out of his hand, he got his wits back in time to catch it before it dropped. "I didn't know you did."

"It's the first time I've been here," she told him. "I was getting tired of the stores I shop at, so I looked in the yellow pages and noticed this place wasn't too far away. Just came to check it out."

Kent nodded. "It's a small store, but it has a nice selection."

Nellie's delicate eyebrows drew together in an earnest expression. "Do you know if they have pickled herring? I can't find it at the other stores."

"Sure. Over here in the deli section." He motioned for her to follow him. "They import it from Sweden. It's excellent."

When they came up to the refrigerated, glass display case, she peered at the tub of gray-white herring pieces curiously. "That's it?" she said, her nose wrinkling slightly.

"I thought you liked it," he said.

Quickly, she looked up at him. "I've never had it, actually. I...I read it's good for dieting. Being fish, it's low-cal. Makes a good snack food. So I thought I'd try it."

"You diet?" he asked, looking down at her small frame. She had one hand in her jeans pocket, pushing back her jacket. Her snugly fit denims showed no sign of plumpness around her waist or hips. Though above the waist, she certainly had more to her than he ever had realized.

At his question, she wet her lips and then chuckled. "My weight is okay. I...just want to keep it that way. I'm trying to get away from junk food."

"That's smart. I eat herring a lot. It makes a nice snack—though some people think it's a little odd."

"How much do you usually buy?" she asked him. The proprietor's wife was walking over to the deli counter, looking as if she wanted to assist them.

"Start with a quarter pound," he suggested. "In case you don't like it."

"Hello, Kent. Can I help either of you?" the lady asked with a smile.

"Hi, Gladys," Kent said. "Where's Burt?"

"Helping our daughter buy a car," the gray-haired lady replied. "He'll be in this afternoon."

"I'd like a quarter pound of the herring," Nellie said.

"Half pound for me," Kent told her.

When Gladys had apportioned and wrapped their herring, Kent took his package of fish, picked up a shopping basket from a stack by the counter and loaded the cereal and herring into it. He carried the red basket over to the bread section to pick out a loaf.

Nellie followed suit and took a basket, then came over to the bread shelves. She selected the same brand as he.

"Do you live near here?" she asked.

"About two blocks away on Cedar," he said. "That's why this place is so convenient. I can just walk over."

"Do you like your apartment? Mine's a studio—

one room basically, with a kitchen area. It's a little small. I'm thinking of looking for a new place, if I can afford it."

"Mine's a two-bedroom condo. The rooms aren't huge, but it's comfortable. I'm planning to sell it, though, and buy a house."

"You're planning to sell? For how much?"

Kent hadn't decided for certain yet, but he mentioned a figure.

"I might be able to swing that by the end of the year. I've been saving and I should be getting a raise soon. When are you moving?"

Kent lifted his shoulders. "I don't know for sure. When I find the right house."

"It sounds like the sort of place I'd like to have. I ought to invest in a condo instead of renting, so I have equity."

"Sounds like you've been doing some financial planning," he said with a smile.

"Yes. And just plain old planning for my future and figuring out what I want. This seems like a nice neighborhood. Have you enjoyed living on Cedar?"

"It's been fine. I just want to invest in a house." He moved over to the refrigerated case displaying milk and orange juice. Again she followed.

"Would you mind if I walk along with you back to your place?" she asked, picking up a quart of orange juice and putting it into her basket. "I'd like to see what your building looks like. You don't have to invite me in or anything. Just want to get an idea of the place so I can keep it in mind."

This threw Kent slightly. Again, he wondered if she was actually pursuing him or if she was simply interested in seeing whether his place suited her as a possible future home. Out of curiosity to see what she was up to, he decided to go along with her suggestion. "Sure, I'll show you my place. Happy to."

"Thanks."

When they'd finished shopping, they stopped at her car briefly to leave her groceries in the back seat. "It's cool enough today that things won't spoil," she said as she locked the door. "I won't be gone long, anyway."

She walked alongside of him down the sidewalk to his street. On the way they made small talk about the office and the coming tax season when everyone would be working overtime. She asked him what his duties in his new position in the Worldwide Division would be.

But all the while they talked shop, Kent was aware of her feminine presence beside him, her short stature making him feel as if he towered over her, making him feel unusually protective toward her. Her graceful way of walking, her long hair billowing away from her fresh face in the breeze gave her a mesmerizing beauty that seemed new to him and quietly alluring. He was used to being around attractive, polished women with perfect makeup and slick hairstyles. But Nellie seemed so natural, gentle and ultrafeminine, that he grew aware again, as he had back at the candy factory, of how strong and thoroughly male he felt beside her. It was a heady sensation, and he couldn't help but relish it—maybe more than he ought to for being a sensible, rational man. She evoked feelings in him that he wasn't sure how to deal with. He didn't like to think there was a possibility that he could go on some emotional tangent that might get out of control.

He gave her a quick tour of his condo building, showing her the small lobby and the laundry room before taking her up to his apartment on the third floor.

"Here it is," he said when he'd unlocked and opened the door. He motioned for her to go in ahead of him into the living room. "I'll show you the kitchen first, since I have to put the groceries away."

She followed him into the small kitchen. He was glad he'd straightened up the place this morning. Her eyes were wide and shining as she looked around. See, he reassured himself, her eyes were always bright, not just when she looked at him. She wasn't chasing him—not the Nellie he knew.

"This is very nice," she said, running her hand over the wooden kitchen cupboards. "Lots of storage space."

"Yeah, there is," he agreed, opening one of the cupboards to put away the new box of cereal. He put the herring, orange juice and milk in the refrigerator, and some frozen dinners into the freezer section.

When he was finished, he turned to her. "Want to see the bedroom?" He was surprised to see a hint of alarm in her eyes.

"Oh...well, sure," she said with a smile. He had the feeling she was covering her discomfort. He'd always sensed she was a proper young woman—rather old-fashioned, in fact. Her reaction put him even more at ease. She certainly hadn't asked to come up to his apartment in order to seduce him!

He showed her his bedroom with its big bed, which

he'd made up rather haphazardly that morning. "Neatness isn't my strong point," he told her apologetically, taking off his coat and hanging it in the closet. He was glad he'd at least hung up his other clothes that morning.

"I like the blue draperies on the window," she said. "Looks nice with the bedspread." She didn't linger in the room, however, and quickly stepped out into the small hallway.

"The other bedroom I use as an office," he said as he guided her to the next room. "It's smaller than the bedroom, but big enough for the desk and bookcases."

"What kind of computer do you have?" she asked, walking over to the desk to look at it more closely.

They talked about computer software and hardware for about ten minutes and then went back into the kitchen.

"Want a cold drink?" he asked. "I've got some sandwich meats and bread, too. Want to have lunch?"

"Really?" Her eyes grew large again. "I don't want to impose."

"You're not. I was just going to eat at home and catch up on my reading." He had a date that evening, but didn't mention that.

"Well, all right," she said, taking off her jacket. She draped it on the back of a kitchen chair. "I guess my groceries will be okay in the car for a while longer. It was parked in the shade."

Kent got out the loaf of bread and the sandwich meats, gave her a jar of mayonnaise, a knife and some plates, and asked her to make the sandwiches. Meanwhile he dished out some of the pickled herring and poured some soft drinks into glasses.

As they worked, he couldn't help but take surreptitious glances at her formfitting sweater. She had an exquisite figure. Did she have an alter ego? Did she always turn herself into a curvaceous sweater girl on the weekends to make up for having to wear business suits all week?

Still, she was nervous in his bedroom. It didn't quite make sense. Usually women would dress as she was now when they wanted to attract men. If they wanted to attract men, they usually weren't afraid of bedrooms.

He and Nellie sat down to eat. They talked some more about work and about the condo and the neighborhood. Though she kept up her part of the conversation, he could sense her growing increasingly shy, and he wondered why. Over the past week, she'd seemed much more outgoing and sure of herself than she used to be, but now she reminded him again of the girl he'd worked with on the candy factory audit.

"Haven't tried the herring yet," he said, pushing the dish closer to her. "Taste it."

Nellie looked at it and swallowed. "Okay." She picked up the serving fork and poked around—a bit distastefully, he thought—until she found the smallest chunk of fish. This she dropped onto her plate and cut in two with her knife. "It's...raw, right?"

"Yes, but it's cured through pickling, so it's safe."

"Uh-huh," she said, pushing it around her plate.

"I take it you don't eat sushi," he joked.

She laughed. "No way."

"You don't have to eat the herring," he said,

though he couldn't help but wonder why she'd bought a quarter pound of it when she clearly disliked raw fish.

"No," she said, sounding firm. "I'll try it." She picked up one of the two tiny pieces on her plate with her fork and lifted it to her mouth.

Kent couldn't help but be amused at the changing expressions on her face. It was like watching a child eat something for the first time. She chewed and swallowed it, looking as though she might live.

"Well," she said, "it's different. The flavor is interesting. I guess a person could acquire a taste for it. The texture of the raw fish is odd, though."

He nodded. "Chewy. You'll get used to it. Have some more."

She glanced at him and smiled. "I'll try it again at home. Are we finished? I'll help with the dishes."

"That's okay. There aren't many."

"No, I want to," she told him. "I didn't expect to get lunch. Thanks."

They both stood up, and as they picked up their dishes and carried them to the sink at the same time, they bumped into each other.

"Oh, sorry," she said as she set her plate and empty glass on the counter. She took a step back so she was no longer in physical contact with him.

Kent's head was spinning slightly and he felt himself growing warm. His arm had accidentally brushed against her breast, and all he could think about was how round and firm her body had felt. The vivid dream he couldn't forget raged into his mind. His dishes rattled as he set them down. She might not be chasing him, but *he* certainly felt like grabbing hold of *her.* He tried to quell his heated impulses, but his usually steadfast willpower didn't seem to be working just now.

"You really look great in that sweater," he said, his voice coming out husky.

She lowered her eyes self-consciously. Looking so sweet it unsettled him even more, she smoothed the sweater with her hands below her breasts downward to where the edge covered the narrow waistband of her jeans. "My sister gave it to me. It's not quite my usual style." She looked up, her brown eyes big and questioning. "You really think it looks okay?"

Her apparent innocence touched him. Was she for real? He'd always preferred sophisticated women, but her unawareness of how damned sexy she looked somehow made her all the more desirable. "Better not wear it to work," he told her, catching his breath. His arm muscles twitched as he yearned to enfold her. He felt nervous and as excited as a racehorse waiting for the starting pistol to go off. "You'll have the men swarming around you."

She laughed, as if she thought he was making a joke. "I doubt th—" she began to say, but stopped abruptly when he took her in his arms. "Kent—" she said, setting her hands against his chest. Her instinctive protective action charmed him even more, and her fingers pressing into his pectoral muscles aroused him as thoroughly as a man can be aroused.

"I try to think of you as a sister. But all of a sudden I don't feel the least bit brotherly. Can't seem to fight it," he said in a rush, keeping her close, gradually lowering his face toward hers.

She took a deep, shaky breath, but did not try to push out of his grasp. "You can't?"

"Crazy, huh?"

"Yeah."

"Let's try…a quick experiment," he said, ignoring the rational side of his conscience telling him he was taking the wrong path.

"Experi—?"

He kissed her before she could finish the word. Her mouth accepted his, indeed quickly fixed on his, and she slid her hands up his shoulders and around his neck. He pulled her closer as he leaned over her, and he felt her sweet, firm breasts pressing into his chest. Heat radiated between them. Her body grew pliant and almost limp as she clung to him, as if all her energy was going into her warm lips as she kissed him back wholeheartedly.

Time and place seemed to vanish. He slid his hands over her back and around to caress the sides of her breasts. His lips left hers and he kissed her neck beneath her ear. She whimpered with pleasure when his hand cupped her breast, pressing his palm into it. He took her response as permission to do more, and he slid his fingers beneath the V neckline of her sweater. The feel of her silky warm skin, the heavy softness of her supple flesh made his breathing grow labored and his heart begin to thud with need. His fingertips found her nipple, and she let out a sharp, aching gasp. Her slender body began to tremble.

"Kent," she said, her voice sounding weak with deep yearning. "Oh, Kent." She leaned her forehead against his chin and drew in her breath, making her breast press more firmly against his fingers, as if she wanted more of the sensations his caresses seemed to provide her. Then she stretched up to kiss his chin and found his mouth again.

He responded hotly, spurred on by her body writhing sensually against his, wondering if he should carry her into the bedroom. But then his rational side finally shouted in his head, *This is Nellie—Nellie Brown!*

He tore his mouth from hers, let her go and stepped back. "Sorry," he said, stunned and out of breath. "I lost my head."

Nellie, her hair mussed and clothes disheveled, looked lost and forsaken. She stood there gazing helplessly at him, shaking. He felt very badly. He hadn't wanted to upset or hurt her. But he had to stop them from…well, he didn't even want to think about what he'd been ready to do with her.

With trembling hands, she pulled her sweater into place and pushed back her hair. Now she looked acutely embarrassed. "I don't usually behave this way," she said, looking down at the floor as if she felt guilty now. "I'm sorry. I didn't mean to…to act like a loose woman."

Her sincerity almost brought tears to his eyes. "I could never think of you as a loose woman, believe me. It's my fault. I took advantage of you. You looked too good in that sweater, and… We're co-workers. I'm the senior employee and I ought to have known better. I never should have let this happen. Don't blame yourself."

She still had that lost look in her wide, glassy eyes. "I'd better go."

"That would probably be best," he agreed.

She picked up her jacket and walked through the living room to the door. He followed, not knowing what to say. When they got to the door, he reached around her to open it. Her shoulder brushed against his chest. They both reflexively jumped away from each other, as though electricity had arced between them.

After catching her breath, Nellie said, "Bye."

"Goodbye," he replied. He looked after her for a moment as she walked down the hall to the elevator, thinking if he were polite, he'd walk down to the street with her or even back to her car. But under the circumstances, it was much safer for him to let her go now. He closed the door.

Kent sat down on his living-room couch for a while, recovering. Despite his erotic dream about her, he'd have never imagined that kissing Nellie in real life could ignite his desire so fast. Usually he took a little more time with a woman. God, he'd started fondling her breast within half a minute!

Even more amazing was the way she'd responded. Nellie always had an innocence about her. In fact, he'd probably have guessed she was a virgin, except that most women these days had their first sex experience by the time they were eighteen or twenty. In any case, he'd never expected her to quiver at his touch with such sweet longing, to writhe against him with such heated desire.

You've got to stop thinking about it, he told himself. It was an accidental incident due to unusual circumstances. If they hadn't run into each other in that grocery store and she hadn't been wearing that sweater, the whole thing never would have happened.

So just pretend it didn't, he instructed himself. Thank goodness he had a statuesque blonde to see tonight. Their second date, too. Maybe things would heat up and she'd make him forget his crazy encounter with Nellie.

Twelve hours later, Kent found himself sitting on the same couch, dressed in a suit and tie now, still stewing about Nellie. He'd gone on the date with the blonde. The date had been rather pleasant, too—dinner and a play at the Goodman Theater. When he'd brought her home and she'd invited him in for coffee, he'd readily said yes. However, a while later when they began to kiss, Kent had felt disappointed, let down—even deprived. Kissing the blonde had not even come close to what he'd experienced that afternoon with Nellie. It had been like drinking flat beer after having tasted the most vibrant, enticing champagne.

Kent had made some excuse and quickly left. And now, home in his living room, he felt pretty damned confused. He'd thought he'd had things all figured out. He'd thought he knew what he wanted, what he was looking for. But now he had no choice but to wonder—what *did* he really want? The perfect corporate wife?

Or Nellie?

# 4

It was one o'clock in the morning and Nellie couldn't
fall asleep. She had driven home that afternoon with
tears streaming down her cheeks, having just lived
through the best and worst experiences she'd ever had
with Kent. Her plan to run into him at the store had
gone perfectly. She'd even gotten him to show her
his condo, a ploy she'd thought of the night before,
though she'd doubted she'd be able to carry it off.
But it had gone beautifully. He seemed to fall easily
into every trap she set.

Until she got caught in her own trap. Her wildest
dreams had come true. He'd kissed her! Kissed her
with passion and ardor. And she—in love with him
for so long—had forgotten herself and allowed all her
pent-up longing to rush out. She'd behaved like a
wanton, on their very first kiss, the very first time
they'd ever been alone together. What must he think
of her?

She should have been the one to stop them from
going further, not him. He probably thought she was
easy, not at all the type of respectable woman a man
would want to marry and become the mother of his
children.

Nellie hadn't known she could behave that way, even with Kent. When he'd shown her his bedroom, she'd felt inhibited, imagining him sleeping in his bed, wondering if he wore pajamas or not, imagining how adorable he must look asleep. Besides all that, she'd never been in a man's bedroom before. She'd tried to appear nonchalant, but she had the feeling he might have noticed her diffidence. While they'd eaten lunch, she'd become aware again of being alone with him, having him all to herself just as she'd always dreamed, and then her innate shyness had come over her and she'd found it difficult to be at ease.

And then, suddenly, he'd taken her in his arms— and she'd turned from a shrinking violet into a Venus's-flytrap. Oh, God, how could she face seeing him on Monday?

On Monday morning, Kent arrived at work early. He phoned a restaurant on Michigan Avenue, across the street from the Art Institute, and made a lunch reservation.

Then he looked out into the office to see if Nellie had come in yet. Her desk was empty.

He paced in his office a bit, hands in his pants pockets, wondering how he should approach the situation. He had to consider that Nellie, after having the weekend to think about the way he'd practically attacked her when she was all alone with him at his condo, might not *want* to have lunch with him. He needed to show her that he could behave like a gentleman. Lunch at a nice place and an hour or so at the Art Institute might help to restore his image.

Usually he took women to the Art Institute to see

how they responded to the atmosphere. He wanted a woman who was at ease with art and music, who didn't look bored at a concert or a museum, a woman with an element of class. And, to be honest, if he wanted such a high-class lady, he needed to show her that he had some sensibility toward art, too. But he'd never taken a woman to the Art Institute before to prove to her that he didn't always behave like King Kong did with Fay Wray in the old movie.

He scratched his eyebrow. It had just occurred to him that Nellie might not be free for lunch. He hoped she was. He felt the need to put their relationship back on an even keel—and yes, relationship was the right word. The pull between them was too strong to ignore. He could never again look upon her as a cousin or sister, not after the way he'd kissed and fondled her.

There had turned out to be a strong sexual attraction between them. How long had that been going on, without his being consciously aware of it? Until he'd had that dream the other night, he hadn't had a clue he desired her. He had the nagging feeling that there might be a lot more going on beneath the surface than just physical chemistry, too. Her ingenuousness, her effortless beauty, her quiet sweetness tugged at his heart in some strange, stirring way he could no longer ignore.

Arnie had a crush on her. So did Rudy. She had something that made strong men melt. Why should Kent be immune? Indeed, if he had so much competition, he'd better get to work.

About twenty minutes later, he saw Nellie walk to her desk with her briefcase. She was wearing one of her gray suits and her hair was pulled back from her face with barrettes again. Kent straightened his tie, took a long breath and walked over.

"Hi," he said quietly, not wanting to startle her, for she was busy sorting through work papers in her briefcase.

She looked up, her beautiful full mouth dropped open, but nothing came out. Her eyes were round with what looked like fright.

"You okay? I didn't mean to sneak up on you. Or...is it me you're scared of?" He held his breath, fearing the worst.

"You? No, I..." She stopped midsentence, sat still, blinking her eyes for a moment. "I'm not afraid of you. Why would I be? I, um, didn't know if you'd want to talk to *me*."

Kent was greatly relieved that she still seemed to have a good opinion of him. "I know we parted kind of abruptly after what happened Saturday. I think we both were a little stupefied. But I've had time to think it over. Maybe you have, too. It seems to me," he said, nervously straightening his tie again, "that there's something rather powerful going on between us that we'd be foolish to ignore."

He could see a responsive flame in her eyes when he'd said the word powerful. Relaxing a bit, sensing that she might be in agreement, he continued. "So, I thought maybe we should start exploring this...this *thing* that's hit us. But perhaps we should go about it slowly this time. I thought we might have lunch today, if you're free." He paused for her answer, holding his breath again, though feeling quite hopeful now.

She smiled, looking shy. "I'm free. I'd like that."

"About eleven? After lunch we can go over to the Art Institute for a while."

Her expression changed to one of apprehension.

"Did you have an appointment with a client today or something? We can just have lunch and do the Art Institute another day, if that suits your schedule better," he offered.

Nellie rubbed her nose. "No. I have appointments tomorrow, but none today. The—the Art Institute would be fine. I haven't been there for a while."

"Great. See you at eleven."

Kent went back to his office whistling under his breath. He ran into Arnie coming from the coffee machine.

"What are you whistling so merrily about on a Monday morning?" Arnie asked, looking as if he needed his coffee to wake up.

"Got a hot date," Kent said.

"A new blonde?"

"No. A shy brunette."

Arnie's expression fell. "Oh. I thought she didn't fit your qualifications list."

"What list?" Kent asked with a grin.

"You mean, the leopard's changed his spots?" Arnie said doubtfully. "You hurt her, you're looking at a knuckle sandwich from me."

Kent stared at him in surprise. "Why would I hurt her? That's the last thing I'd want to do."

"I don't think you know what you want, despite all your plans and your list. And if you've thrown out your list, it probably means you're even more mixed up than you were. Now you don't even have artificial guidelines to follow.''

"I'm paying attention to my feelings," Kent said, "something I realize I haven't done for a long time."

"Your feelings? So now you're on Mr. Toad's Wild Ride. Where will you be when the ride ends? You're all ambition, Kent. You have no rudder. If you hurt a vulnerable young woman because you take the ride and then take a hike, I won't have any more respect for you."

With that, Arnie walked off, spilling some of his coffee onto the office carpeting. Kent didn't know what to make of his friend's huffy speech. He could only assume that it grew out of jealousy, because Arnie had been hoping to date Nellie himself. Kent felt badly, but also felt there was nothing he could do. Arnie wasn't the type to stay angry for long, anyway.

After turning in the final report to her superior for the audit she'd completed last week, Nellie unzipped a compartment in her handbag. She pulled out some notes she'd taken several days ago from a library book on the Impressionist painters. She'd hoped she'd have more time to study them in the event that Kent ever asked her to the Art Institute. Now that the event had suddenly happened, she only had a short time to try to memorize her notes.

Gosh, what a shock to have Kent ask her to lunch this morning, after she'd worried all weekend that he'd probably do his best to avoid her. He'd hinted that he thought things had happened too fast, and he seemed to blame himself. He'd even thought she might be afraid of him. She was a little afraid of the strong passion that had flamed so suddenly between them, never having experienced it before. But how could she be afraid of Kent, when the poor man kept falling into every snare she set?

Now, here she was, surreptitiously studying up on the French painters, so she could impress Kent with her "knowledge" of art. She'd ordered several Monopoly games from a catalog, had pretended an interest in the Cubs, jazz, winter and other subjects she either couldn't care less about or downright hated, all to make Kent think she and he were perfect for each other. Well, they *were* perfect together, but not for the superficial mutual interests she'd invented.

Nellie's biggest fear was that one day she'd slip up so badly that he'd see through her. And then what? Would he despise her for pretending, for stretching the truth and telling him fibs to lure him to her? She felt like such a sneak.

But it was working. All's well that ends well, she tried to tell herself. She'd better not stop now, when success seemed just around the corner.

At eleven Kent came by her desk and they left the office. He took her to a very nice restaurant off of Michigan Avenue. After ordering, they talked about Kent's move in a few days to the thirty-fourth floor. She could tell he was excited about it.

"I'll miss running into you, though," he said, reaching across the table to touch her hand.

"So will I," she replied, a bit breathless. She lifted her fingers to touch his in response.

He laced his fingers into hers. "Even though things got a little out of hand on Saturday, I'm glad what happened happened. I'm glad I didn't move up to

Worldwide without discovering the potent chemistry you and I seem to have together.''

"So am I," she said with feeling, not having to fake any sincerity on this point. His large hand fondling her smaller one, his fingers mingling intimately with hers, excited her and she had to work to keep her composure. She longed to be in his arms again.

His blue eyes took on an ardent glow. "It's a good thing we're in a public place, or I'm afraid I'd be tempted to do a lot more than hold your hand. Just feeling your fingers between mine turns me on so much I have a hard time thinking straight."

Nellie smiled and looked down. "I know what you mean."

"I didn't know a shy woman could be so sexy."

She laughed softly and couldn't look at him. "Me, either. I never felt sexy until—" she bravely met his warm, searching eyes "—until Saturday when you...when all that happened. I don't usually behave that way."

"I believe you. I don't usually behave that way, either—not that fast, anyway. It just shows that we've got something special going on here." He glanced down for a moment. "Even back at the candy factory, I was aware of something untapped between us. I...just didn't think we were right for each other back then, so I ignored it." He smiled at her. "I've wised up."

Nellie bit her lip, wondering how much she should reveal about her own feelings. "I remember." She shook her head in a self-deprecating manner. "I had a crush on you. I imagine you knew," she said, feeling her cheeks grow hot with embarrassment.

"I didn't want to know," Kent replied with gentleness. "I convinced myself you were too shy to have a crush on anyone. But you know what? With all the predatory women out there nowadays, it's a relief to be with a girl who's too shy to chase a man, even one she really likes. I'm so much more relaxed with you than with some of the wily females I've met and even dated. Too bad we've wasted all this time."

Nellie gulped hard, trying to swallow her deep sense of guilt. "Yes, it's too bad," she agreed. And it was. If he'd only asked her out after the candy factory audit, she'd never have had any reason to resort to stratagems to win him. Now she had a secret to keep from Kent, the one person in the world with whom she most wanted to be free and honest.

After lunch, they walked across Michigan Avenue to the Art Institute, an impressive stone building with colorful flags and two huge sculptured lions on each side of its entrance steps. They left their coats in the coat-check room and walked up the large elaborate staircase to the second floor. She wasn't surprised when he led her into the halls featuring paintings by the French Impressionists. The Art Institute had a large collection of paintings by Renoir, Monet, Seurat, and others.

She paused as they passed by the famous Seurat painting, *A Sunday on La Grande Jatte,* depicting people in a grassy park relaxing on a Sunday afternoon.

Nellie smiled, remembering seeing this painting at different points in her life since childhood. "I'm always amazed at how big this painting is. It almost takes up the whole wall."

"It is impressive. The style is so unusual, done with points of color instead of regular brush strokes."

"Yes, he was the most famous of the Pointillistes," she said, quoting from the notes she'd studied earlier.

"That's right, pointillism. I'd forgotten the name."

"He used dots of primary colors that blend together when looked at from a distance," Nellie continued. "It produces a luminous effect."

Kent nodded. "I like this painting, but on the whole, I guess I like Monet and Renoir better."

"I agree." It was becoming a habit to agree with everything he said, Nellie noticed. In a way, she'd stopped thinking for herself. Well, it was working. Don't blow it now by worrying about it. If she managed to marry Kent, she could start thinking again when the wedding was over.

She realized there was something pretty askew about her reasoning. She was rationalizing her behavior. But Kent was moving on to the next room, and she had to be on the ball. No time to analyze herself now.

They stood in front of a large painting by Caillebotte, called *Paris Street: Rainy Day*. It showed a cobblestone street, wet with rain, brightly reflecting the pale gray of the overcast sky. A man and a woman in late nineteenth-century clothing were in the foreground of the picture, walking down a sidewalk with big umbrellas over their heads. City buildings were in the background.

"The perspective in this painting is amazing," Kent commented. "The people with the umbrellas are actually life-size and the buildings in the background really look like they're off in the distance. It's painted so well, you feel like you could step into the picture and walk down that wet street.''

"Yes," she agreed, truly feeling what he'd described. However, he'd thrown her a bit by mentioning the word perspective. It was an art term she hadn't looked up. She decided to stick with what she'd studied. "I like the way he illustrated light in this picture. That's what Impressionism is—painting the impression of light. Monet said, 'Light is the principal person in the picture.' This certainly demonstrates that—the shiny street and the bright, diffused light it reflects just…just make this picture shine.'' She knew she'd gotten the quote right, but the rest was all improvised.

He turned to her, his eyes pleasingly alert. "You know a lot about art. I'm impressed! No pun intended," he joked. "I'm a novice compared to you."

"No, not really. I…just read a book once," she assured him. She didn't want him to conclude she was some kind of art expert, because she'd never be able to live up to that image.

As they continued down the halls, viewing painting after painting, he said, "It's amazing how productive the Impressionists were."

"Especially since the movement only lasted twenty years," she chimed in, reciting more from her notes.

"That's all?" he asked, surprised.

"The movement split up because the various artists evolved different ideas. Some took the scientific approach using dots of color. Others went into color symbolism." Whatever that was. Nellie again was recalling what she'd read. "The artists didn't see eye to eye anymore. Their theories and paintings were scoffed at during their lifetimes. They all were poor and suffered miserably.''

She stopped, realizing that Kent was looking at her with the most tender gaze she'd ever seen.

"You're adorable," he said. "You have such sweet sensitivity." He slipped his arm around her waist and pulled her close. "You're too good for me."

"No, I'm not," she tried to say, but he shushed her.

"Don't argue. Just kiss me."

She smiled. "But there are some people over in the other corner of the room," she whispered.

"They won't mind. Love is an art form, too. Kiss me." He bent his head toward hers and kissed her gently. She readily gave in to his embrace as his statement about love echoed in her brain. Was he hinting that he loved *her?* Oh, God. Was it too good to be true?

As they ended the kiss, she tried to keep calm and not reflect too much on what he'd said. It might have only been a little quip on his part, not meant to convey anything. But just the fact that he was openly kissing her in a public place indicated he wasn't hiding his feelings toward her.

They left the art museum to go back to the office. Nellie felt relieved. She'd about run out of nifty pieces of info on Impressionism. When they reached their building, they got onto an empty elevator and pressed the button for the twentieth floor. As soon as the doors closed, Kent took her in his arms again. He kissed her soundly and she responded with equal fervor. Despite the bulky winter coats they were wearing, the physical chemistry between them made things heat up fast.

They broke the kiss only when they felt the elevator coming to a stop.

Nellie laughed breathlessly, raising her fingertips to her lips, hoping her lipstick wasn't too smeared. "I thought you said we were going to take it slow."

As the doors opened, Kent smiled at her and in a rueful tone said, "I did. I meant it, too. But I'm beginning to wonder how long 'slow' can last."

# 5

Several days later, Nellie helped Kent move his things up to the thirty-fourth floor. She was sad to see him leave the twentieth floor, but not as sad as she might have been had she not bought *How To Marry Your Dreamboat* and followed the book's advice. Now she was the current woman in his life, and if she didn't see him during the day, she knew she would see him most evenings. They'd begun having dinner together after work, going to a restaurant in the Loop or on the Near North Side where they both lived. They were long, lingering dinners, followed by long, lingering kisses at her door.

So far, she hadn't invited him in, and he hadn't seemed to expect her to. Apparently he meant to keep his promise to take their romance at a slow pace. This was fine with her. She had the feeling that if they were ever alone together for too long, she might find herself in an intimate situation with him that she wasn't sure she was ready for.

He'd had lots of girlfriends, that much was common knowledge. And she wasn't naive enough to assume that many of those women hadn't offered him sex as a tactic to get close to him. She remembered

Kent mentioning the predatory women he'd met and how comfortable he felt with Nellie because she wasn't that way. Though she was willing to tell fibs and pretend she liked everything he liked, she instinctively drew the line at using sex as a strategy.

It was an easy line to draw, since she wouldn't know how to use sex to lure a man even if she wanted to. That was the problem with being a virgin.

Would he mind her lack of experience if the time ever came? She hoped not. After all the effort she'd made to get him to notice her and then date her, she hoped she wouldn't lose him because she didn't know how to please him in bed. It quickly occurred to her that there were lots of books constantly being published about how to have great sex. Maybe she could learn that from a book, too.

She went to the bookstore and bought three.

After reading the sex manuals over the next several nights before going to bed, Nellie felt both tantalized and anxious. While she longed to have her first experience with Kent, she worried that she'd fumble and forget what she'd learned in the books and disappoint him with her unpracticed technique. But the books had educated her enough to do one thing—she went out and bought condoms, so she'd be prepared. She wasn't stupid enough to let herself get pregnant by the man she loved, not when she wasn't married to him yet.

One Saturday night, after spending the afternoon with Kent at the Lincoln Park Zoo and having dinner with him at a restaurant, he took her home. It was earlier than usual and he looked as though he didn't really want to say good-night yet. She didn't want to, either.

"Would you like to come in for a while?" she asked.

"Should we risk being alone together?" he said, eyes twinkling.

"Why not?" she replied, trying to sound unconcerned, though her heart was already beginning to beat faster.

They took off their jackets and she hung them up in the small closet near the door. She quickly glanced at the refrigerator door to make sure she'd taken down the columnar sheet she often had posted there. "Would you like something to drink?" she asked.

"No," he said, looking around. Until now, he'd only glimpsed her small place.

The problem with a one-room studio apartment was that the living room was also the bedroom. Her daybed, made up with a terra-cotta and jade green bedspread and big matching pillows against its high-backed oak frame, also served as her living-room couch. There were two jade upholstered chairs facing it with a small oak table between them.

"Where do you sleep?" he asked, eyeing the daybed.

"There. If you take off all the big pillows, it's actually a twin bed."

"I see."

He sat down on a chair and she took the other chair. Both avoided looking at the bed now. Nellie wished she wasn't so nervous. She had the feeling she might be making him nervous, too.

He reached across the small table between the

chairs to take her hand. "Don't worry. It's not my intention to try anything serious. I like the way we've been doing things. I feel I'm getting to know you."

She smiled. "I'm not worried—just not used to having a man here." And then she realized she was admitting a certain lack of experience.

"You haven't dated much?"

"I dated in college. Since I've been working and moved in here, I...no, I haven't. Haven't had time," she said, making an excuse.

"How long have you lived here?"

"About six months."

"Where did you live before that?"

She rolled her eyes. "At home in the suburbs with my parents."

He chuckled. "Sounds like you were glad to get out on your own."

"You can't imagine. I love my parents, but I never feel very confident when I'm around them. They always compare me to my fabulous sister, and in their eyes, I always come up lacking."

"It must be tough to have a gold-medal winner as a sibling. I was fortunate. I'm an only child. My parents believe the sun rises and sets with me." He inhaled deeply. "But that's not really a good thing, either. Sometimes I think it creates a false sense of reality. I worry that my life's been too easy."

"That must be a nice worry to have," she said with a chuckle.

"You want to trade?" he said, squeezing her hand.

As she laughed, he gently pulled on her arm, as if he wished her to come closer. She realized he wanted her to sit on his lap. Nellie didn't hesitate. She wanted to be closer to him, too.

Both were wearing denims, and as she sat on his lap, her blue jeans slid over his.

"We're such a matched pair," he said. "Even down to our clothes."

"No," she sweetly disagreed. "You've got on a plaid shirt, and I've got on a sweater."

"Not your famous apricot one, though," he said, fingering the edge of her white short-sleeved pullover. "The one that almost got us into trouble. I notice you've never worn it again."

She smiled and lowered her eyes. "You think I should?"

"Whether you should or not is a whole other question." He nuzzled the side of her face with his nose and his voice was growing low, soft and tantalizingly intimate. "I'm just wondering why you haven't."

Her breaths came faster and she had trouble keeping her thoughts from going astray. "I don't know," she said, nuzzling him back.

"Afraid I'll attack you again?"

"Would you, if I wore it?" she asked, instinctively using a teasing tone of voice.

"Would you want me to?" he asked, biting her ear.

"Whether I would want you to or not is a whole other question," she mimicked him. "I'm asking you if that's what you would do."

He laughed and took hold of her shoulders to give her a little shake. "Are you bandying words with me?"

"Are you answering my question?"

"What's the question?"

"I don't know," she said, laughing. "I lost track."

"Something about the apricot sweater," he murmured, pushing her long hair aside with his hand to kiss her neck. He pulled her closer as his mouth languidly slid to the delicate skin beneath her ear.

She closed her eyes at the sensation and couldn't speak for a moment. "I don't think we need the apricot sweater," she said in a breathless voice. "Things seem to be heating up without it." She gasped when she felt his hand cup her breast.

"It's your gorgeous curves that turn me on, not what's covering them." He tested her softness with the palm of his hand, then paused. "We said we wouldn't do this. Do you want me to stop?"

She closed her eyes, wishing he hadn't stopped. "I like the way you touch me," she whispered.

He caressed her again and his lips found her mouth. She wound her arms around his neck and ran her fingers through his dark, thick hair as she responded to his kiss. It lasted more than a minute, and both were out of breath when they broke the kiss. Her sweater had ridden up as she raised her arms and his hands slid down to the bared skin above the waistband of her jeans. She grew light-headed at the feel of his warm hands on her flesh. As he continued to slide his hands upward, pushing the sweater with it, she didn't object.

When he reached her breasts, she hesitated only a second before cooperating as he pulled the sweater up over her head and tossed it onto the empty chair. Beneath she wore a new lace bra, low-cut and quite sexy.

"You're so beautiful, Nellie," he whispered, running his fingers over her plump cleavage, pushed up by the bra.

His compliment thrilled her, made her catch her breath. She'd longed to be attractive to him.

He began kissing her sensitive skin above the lace, and she smiled with pleasure. When he began pushing down one strap, she did not object, but instead began to breathe harder in anticipation. As the lace slipped off her nipple, exposing her, she gasped with desire. With a new urgency he pressed his hand beneath her breast to bring her hardening nipple closer to his mouth.

He fixed his lips on it hotly, causing a charged sensation to surge through her body. "Oh," she whimpered in helpless response, writhing closer to him. "Oh, Kent..."

Quickly he unsnapped her bra in the back and slipped it off. His mouth found her other breast, and she threw her head back, filled with the joy of feeling more sensually excited than she'd ever dreamed she could. With all the books about foreplay and sex she'd read, nothing had prepared her for the sheer thrill of it, the mad sensations coursing through her body.

He lifted his head and kissed her mouth again, his lips so hot, his whole body so heated, that she had the sensation of melting into him. His hands slid up under her arms and he held her away from him so he could look into her face.

"I'm sorry," he said in a husky voice. "I want to love you. I need to make love with you. We can't go slow anymore."

She nodded, her heart absolutely pounding. "I know. I—I want you to."

"You're sure?"

"Yes. I b-bought condoms."

His eyes widened slightly and he smiled. "You did?"

"It seemed inevitable that this would happen. I wanted to be prepared," she explained, hoping that he didn't think that because she had them that she was too eager.

"Smart girl," he said. "I put one in my wallet—just in case."

She chuckled at him. "So you didn't really think we'd take it slow, did you?"

"I wanted to. But I was afraid I couldn't keep away from you much longer." A subtle fire came into his eyes. "Do you know I dream about you? I lie alone in bed and think about you, and then when I fall asleep, I have the sexiest dreams about you."

She swallowed. "I hope the real thing is as good as your dreams."

The fire in his blue eyes turned to adoration. "I'm sure it'll be even better. Are you worried?"

She bowed her head. "Well..."

He angled his head to one side. "Nellie, you...you aren't a virgin, are you?"

Abruptly she looked up at him, her heart seeming to stop.

"No, I didn't think so," he said apologetically. "You couldn't be. You're what, twenty-four?"

She nodded. "Why?"

"Well, in your eyes I sometimes see a look that...you look a little lost, like getting physical is new to you. On the other hand, you respond with such abandon.''

Nellie bit her lower lip and felt tears welling in her eyes. She wished she were a good enough actress to fib about her lack of sexual experience, but she knew she couldn't carry it off. It was too physical, too real, not like spouting off a few cold facts about French painters or pretending to like winter weather.

She blinked back the tears. "I am a virgin," she said.

He stared at her with widening, amazed eyes.

"The reason I respond this way is because, with you, I forget myself—my usual sense of propriety." Despite her efforts to curb her emotion, a tear rolled down her cheek. "The truth is, I like you so much, and have for so long, that when I'm with you I just…I just want you and that's all I think about. I don't mean to behave like some brazen wanton."

He wiped away the tear and smiled. "A brazen wanton? You're like a sweet, uninhibited nymph. You're just who you are, untouched by the world, authentic and true. I'm glad you felt you could be honest with me and tell me that you're a virgin. Did you think I would mind?"

She nodded.

"I don't. I think you're the most beautiful woman in the world. Why would I mind being the first man in your life?" He brushed his nose playfully against hers. "See? We should always be this honest with each other. It makes all the worries fade away."

He kissed her tenderly, but she felt new tears stinging her eyes, knowing she hadn't been this honest with him for weeks. Her guilty worries quickly faded, however, as their kiss grew steamy and his hands found her breasts again. Soon his fingers unfastened the button on her waistband and he unzipped her jeans. He slid his hand beneath her bikini panties until he found her body's most sensitive spot.

"Ohh…" she groaned as a new sensation coursed through her limbs.

"You're ready, aren't you?" he whispered urgently. "So am I. Let's toss those pillows off the bed."

Her head was swimming with desire and apprehension of the unknown. She stood and walked with him the few steps to the daybed. He began throwing off the decorative pillows, clearing the bed except for one pillow. Next he tore off his clothes. She followed suit by removing her jeans and shoes. She left her panties, however, still too inhibited to deal with that just yet.

When she saw his naked masculinity she lost her balance, or perhaps grew slightly dizzy—she wasn't sure. All she knew was that she had to sit down on the bed. She'd read about men's anatomical parts, but seeing things with her own eyes was a whole different experience.

Kent's eager eyes softened. "You doing okay?"

"Just a little dizzy," she said. "You look so… powerful."

He seemed pleased. "I'll take that as a compliment." He paused to pull his wallet out of his discarded jeans. Opening a compartment, he pulled out a condom. Nellie was glad he had the presence of mind to remember—she'd already forgotten about using one, though she'd bought a box.

"Don't be afraid," he said as he approached her,

ripping the small packet open. "I want you to enjoy this, so you'll want to go on making love with me. If I hurt you or make you uncomfortable without knowing it, then tell me. And you can tell me when you like what I'm doing, too. Okay?"

As he slowly stroked her arm, she calmed down. "Okay. W-what happens first?"

"First, I put this on," he said, applying the condom. "Now, lie back on the pillow."

As she did, he placed his hands at her hips and smoothly pulled off her panties. She didn't mind anymore. She felt ready. When he'd thrown the panties onto the rest of her clothes on the chair, he lay down beside her on the bed. Leaning his body over hers, he began to kiss her, gently at first, but then, very soon, the inevitable heat ignited again. He fondled her breasts and slid his hand between her thighs, arousing her until her hips began to undulate with aching need.

"Kent," she breathed in a husky whisper.

"Do you like this?"

"*Ohh,* yes," she moaned. She gasped as his deft caresses caused heightened sensations to steal through her body and tease her endurance. "But...do something...soon."

He moved over her, causing her thighs to part. As she lay back and closed her eyes, she could feel him probing her softness. And then she felt the length of him sliding deep inside. She experienced a tightness. It hurt a little. But then she relaxed, and as he undulated his pelvis, the sensation of him inside her brought tears of exquisite pleasure to her eyes.

"This is beautiful," she whispered, wrapping her

arms around his strong body. "I never felt anything like this."

"I know," he said softly, his mouth near her ear. "I don't think I've felt quite like this ever before, either. You're so special, Nellie. So darling and sweet. There's no one else like you. I want you forever."

New tears slid back from her eyes into her hair. His words and the way he'd said them were so poignant and meant so much to her. She'd always thought making love with Kent would be wonderful, but she hadn't imagined it would be this emotional and meaningful. And so terribly intimate. She felt as if they were one, not only physically, but that their very souls were blending.

As their lovemaking continued, the sensations in her body grew stronger, more torrid, more demanding. His body rocked with hers in a rhythmic heat, until she was gasping for breath. Instinctively she brought her legs up across his back to intensify the sensation. Soon she was crying out with each forward thrust, feeling delirious with pleasurable need.

All at once, a new tension inside her made her draw in her breath sharply in a high, singing sound. She cried out as her body suddenly convulsed in voluptuous spasms while she clung to him. Deep contractions in her lower stomach released the pent-up physical tension. In the midst of her own ecstasy, she felt his body tighten with pleasure inside her as he made a final, forceful thrust.

And then their bodies relaxed in mutually felt fulfillment. He remained on top of her for a full minute, while both caught their breath, returning to normal. Nellie had never felt so contented, so complete.

Kent disentangled his body from hers and lay next to her on his side, looking down at her. He stroked her face and hair. "You're wonderful. You're a dream lover. I'm glad you're mine." His eyes grew moist. "I never knew I could feel this way about anyone."

"I'm so happy," she told him. "I'm thrilled I made you happy, too."

"You have." He reached to pick up a pillow from the floor and, sitting up on the bed, he put the pillow behind him against the bed's oak frame back. He looked as if he wanted to talk. Following his lead, she sat up, too, leaning against the pillow that had been under her head.

"You know," he said with a smile, "I think you've changed my life."

She studied his shining eyes. "I have?"

"I'm afraid I had certain ideas about what I wanted in a woman. But you've gotten under my skin, and now I can't even remember what I thought I wanted. I feel like myself with you, not like I'm playing some kind of elaborate game with someone. I know instinctively that I can trust you because you're so honest about yourself, about everything."

"Oh." Nellie bowed her head. Her hands grew cold.

"You don't know how grateful I am to have found you. You're like a hidden treasure I've discovered, a new truth I've learned about life. And we have so much in common, too, so many mutual interests. I think I've found my soul mate."

Nellie had wrapped her arms around her rib cage, feeling chilled and a little sick. She could no longer look at him.

"Are you cold?" he asked with concern. "Maybe you'd better put on some clothes."

"Yes," she said, eager to have a reason to move off the bed.

She went to the closet and pulled out her long quilted robe. While she slipped it on, he grabbed his jeans and put them back on. As she slowly walked back, he was buttoning his shirt. She sat on a chair instead of the bed. He seated himself on the bed again, but leaned forward, his elbows on his knees.

"As I was saying," he continued eagerly, "what we have together is so incredibly real and authentic that I think we should make it permanent. I know you have feelings for me. And as for me, well, I fell in love—"

"Kent." She interrupted before he could speak further. "There's—there's something you should know."

He straightened up. "Something I should know?" he repeated, looking puzzled. He smiled. "You have some deep dark secret?"

She brushed her trembling fingertips across her mouth, now as dry as cotton, wishing she didn't feel compelled to confess to him that their relationship wasn't as real and authentic as he believed. "This is hard for me," she said, her voice beginning to shake.

His brows drew together in empathy. "You can tell me anything. You know that."

She nodded. "I hope you can understand. I didn't

mean any harm. But...remember how we got along
at the candy factory?''

"Of course."

"That's when I fell in love with you. But after that
audit was over, you didn't pay any further attention
to me."

"I was stupid—"

"Let me finish. Please. This is so hard to tell you.
When I heard you were moving up to the thirty-fourth
floor, I...I panicked. I was afraid I'd lose any chance
with you. I did a...a sort of crazy thing. I bought a
book."

"Book?"

She turned and pulled open the small drawer in the
table next to her. Taking out the book, she reluctantly
showed him its cover.

*"How To Marry Your Dreamboat,"* he read aloud.
He looked slightly uneasy now. "And?"

"I read it and followed its advice. One thing it
suggested was to find out what the man you want
likes and then develop an interest in those things. I
only had two weeks. I didn't have time to develop a
true interest in the Cubs or the Impressionists or any
of the list of things Arnie told me you enjoyed. I
could only pretend—"

"Arnie? A list?"

She swallowed. "I took Arnie to lunch, knowing
that you're his best friend at the office. I got him to
tell me all about your personal interests. I took notes.
I even made up a work sheet—" She got up from the
chair, went to her small desk in the corner where her
computer was and opened a drawer. She pulled out
the yellow columnar sheet she once had posted

on the refrigerator door. Unfolding it, she walked back to her chair and handed it to him. "I listed each thing you liked, when I mentioned it in front of you, your reaction, and I rated my...my success."

Kent's blue eyes darkened as he looked over the sheet. "I don't understand. I don't get why you did this."

"I pretended to like everything you liked, so you would think I was the perfect woman for you. I made sure to say something about each subject in front of you—like the argument with Arnie about the billy goat curse. I wanted you to think I was interested in the Cubs. I'm not. I couldn't care less about baseball. And all that stuff I spouted off about the Impressionists. I got that from a library book I borrowed."

"And you rated your success? What is this, a scale of one to ten?"

"Yes. I thought that way I could keep track of my progress."

"I see you gave yourself a ten on the Impressionists," he muttered sardonically.

"You seemed to hang on every word I said. And you kissed me, right there in the Art Institute."

"By then, you knew you had me in the palm of your hand." His voice had grown tense. He tossed the yellow sheet onto the floor as if filled with contempt for it.

"Kent, I'm sorry. I know you trusted me, and now I've broken that trust. But I couldn't let you propose to me without—"

"Propose?" he interrupted. "What makes you think I was going to propose?"

She knew he'd been about to ask her to marry him.

Apparently he felt the need to save face. An icy chill washed through her, and she didn't answer his question. She realized that in confessing her organized campaign to win him she was probably losing him forever. "What more can I say to apologize to you, Kent? If I'd been sensible, I might have foreseen that my scheme would backfire on me. But I didn't know what else to do. I was so in love—"

"Don't try to dignify this with talk about love," he said in a hoarse voice.

Tears streamed down her cheeks. What more could she do? How could she repair the damage? "But I *do* love you," she insisted desperately. "Is there any way you can ever forgive me?"

# 6

Kent stared at Nellie in disbelief. She'd just stuck a knife in his heart, and now she wanted to know if he could ever forgive her? "No," he said, feeling his throat close up with emotion. He used all his willpower to keep control of himself. "Forgive your calculated sincerity? Your lies? Your scheming innocence?" He felt thoroughly disillusioned and betrayed. The true, pure love he'd thought he'd miraculously discovered with her was only a grand, well-planned manipulation on her part. "I'm supposed to forgive you for setting me up and making a fool out of me?"

"I'm so ashamed, Kent. I feel terrible about what I did. I didn't do it to make a fool of you. I did it because I cared about you so much."

"Oh, that's a sterling reason to set a trap. And I almost fell into it, didn't I? God, I've been stupid to believe you were so sweet and naive. I didn't have a clue I was in the hands of an expert con artist."

She burst into tears again. He could almost believe she was really sorry. Maybe she was. But how could he ever trust her again? All the love and tenderness he'd felt for her only a few minutes ago had vanished.

She was a she-wolf in lamb's clothing. Sorry or not, she'd never have an opportunity to toy with him again!

Through her sobs she said, "I know you must hate me. B-but please at least say you'll forgive me?"

He stood and glowered down at her. "No, I can't forgive you. Not for this."

His jaw set, he walked to the closet and got his jacket. As he grasped the knob of her front door, she ran up to him and pulled on his hand.

"Don't leave yet. Let's talk about it some more," she begged.

He whipped his hand away from hers. "I don't intend to ever talk to you again," he said, keeping his tone quiet and taut, so as not to chance letting his voice break. "Goodbye." With that, he walked through the door and let it slam shut.

As he strode down the hall to the elevator, he glanced behind him, in case she tried to follow him to beg him to come back. But she didn't. Thank God, he told himself. He was well rid of that treacherous little schemer.

How could he have been so unsuspecting? he asked himself incredulously as he drove home. Now that he thought back on various incidents, he could see what she'd meant about bringing up his favorite topics whenever he'd been nearby. When she'd come over to the coffee machine to talk to him about jazz, for example. And when she'd run into him at the grocery store. Indeed, arranging to run into him at Gable's had probably been the mainspring of her trap, her pièce de résistance.

Now that he recalled those incidents, he remembered the thought crossing his mind that she might be chasing him. But she'd been so convincingly artless and innocent that he'd quickly dismissed his suspicions. With each ploy she'd devised, he'd sunk deeper and deeper into the palm of her hand.

And tonight she'd slept with him for the first time, so she'd have an even stronger hold on him, so he'd never want to leave. It had almost worked. He *had* been about to ask her to marry him. And then, for some damned reason, she'd decided to come clean and confess. Why, when her scheme had worked so well? Was it all a game with her? Did she enjoy capturing men, like bumblebees in a net, and then let them go because it was no fun once they were caught?

Naturally she'd claimed she was sorry, tears and sobs and all, and begged for forgiveness. But he didn't believe her repentance was real. Why should he? Nothing else in her character had turned out to be real.

At least he'd gotten free of her net. He might have married her! God, he'd escaped by the skin of his teeth.

After he'd slammed the door in her face, Nellie had shrunk back to the nearest chair and collapsed onto it in shuddering sobs. What had she been thinking, believing that she could win him with such dishonesty? Now she'd lost his respect forever. He'd never love a woman he couldn't respect and trust. Worse, how could she respect herself?

Wiping the wetness from her eyes so she could see, she searched for the book. It was there next to her chair on the small table. In a fit of anger, she picked it up, tore out as many pages as she could until she cut her finger on the edges of the paper, then threw the book across the room.

She wished she'd never seen it in the bookstore, never read it and followed its advice. She'd fallen under its influence to such an extent that she'd forgotten her own sense of right and wrong.

With chagrin, she recalled why she'd put it back on the shelf the first time she'd picked it up—because she felt love should happen naturally. She'd been right in the first place. Using a calculated scheme to win a man won you nothing in the end.

After a dismal sigh, she looked at her bleeding finger and went to the bathroom to wash her hands. As she found the box of bandages in her medicine chest, a new thought came to her. Love with Kent never did come naturally. It had only happened, briefly, while she was pretending to be someone she wasn't—an upstart who knew all about art, the Cubs and wanted to learn about jazz. Kent had never loved her for who she really was.

As she wrapped the bandage around her forefinger, she asked herself, *Why didn't I have more respect for myself? Why did I compromise my own character to get a husband?* She'd be better off staying single than to scheme to get a mate who would only love the woman she made him believe she was and not her true self. Why didn't she wait until some guy on a white horse rode up who said he adored her just as she was, shy, ignorant about music and art and, yes, naive? She must be naive if she thought she could catch a man by following the advice of a stupid book.

Arnie seemed to like her, flaws and all. She didn't

have to put on any pretenses to attract him. Rudy, too. She didn't love either of them, but still, it showed that there were men in the world who could appreciate a diminutive, diffident brunette. Maybe someday she'd meet one that she could fall for.

She doubted she'd ever be able to love another man as much as she did Kent, though. He would always be her first love, the one for whom she'd so willingly given up her virginity. But it had been a big mistake to love him as much as she had.

Her stomach tightened as a new wave of emotion swept over her. She sat down limply on the edge of the small bathtub, tears streaming down her cheeks again. No other man would ever make love to her the way he had. At least she had that one beautiful experience. She might never have another.

By Monday, Nellie had put things straight in her mind, and she was surprisingly composed. After spending the morning at a client's working on an audit, she was walking back to the office just before noon. Having the opportunity to think about herself again as she headed toward her building, she recalled the conclusions she'd come to the night before, reminding herself to remember them.

First, she was going to forget all about Kent. If he hadn't found it in his heart to love her as she was, if he couldn't forgive her for one mistake, however major, then to hell with him!

Second, there were plenty of men in Chicago. It was one city that had a good population ratio of men versus women. She was fortunate to live here. And with Arnie and Rudy already showing interest in her, she did not have far to look to find other fish in the sea. She did not intend to wither away and die as if she were some wallflower because of Kent. Nellie was ready to go out with the first decent man who asked her.

Third, she vowed to work harder at discovering herself and her own interests. All her life, she'd been afraid to be herself, afraid that others would be as unimpressed with her as her parents were. If Kent, or her parents, or anyone else for that matter, found her lacking in some way—too bad! From now on, Nellie would be who she was, nothing more and nothing less. She would please only herself and let the pieces fall where they may.

Bolstered by her resolutions, she walked into the lobby of her building with a feeling of confidence. As she headed for her usual elevator, she passed the other elevator that serviced the top floors of the building. Its doors opened and a group of people got off. In an instant, from the corner of her eye, she realized that Kent was one of them. Should she look at him, or keep walking straight ahead as if she hadn't seen him?

It was like passing a bad accident on the highway. She didn't want to look—but she did. Actually it would have been hard to avoid him, for their predetermined paths crossed rather closely.

Kent's eyes focused on her face and his steps slowed, as if he was thinking about his options, too. They stared at each other for a half second. Then his blue eyes turned icy, his jaw tightened and his mouth, the mouth that had kissed her so tenderly, flattened into a grim line. He looked away and changed his path so as to completely avoid her.

Nellie lowered her gaze, kept herself on a smooth course toward her elevator and congratulated herself on her cool self-control. Once on the elevator, however, after the doors had closed and Kent was safely out of view, her shoulders slumped with relief. She couldn't help but be glad that he worked on the thirty-fourth floor now, and that crossing his path in the lobby occasionally was all she'd ever see of him.

She got off on the twentieth floor, walked to her desk, and set down her heavy briefcase. As she was taking off her coat and hat, Arnie came by.

"Hi. How's it going?" he asked.

"Okay," she said, managing a smile.

"Just okay?" He eyed her more closely. "You look a little pale."

She chuckled dryly. "I saw a ghost on my way to the elevator."

Arnie feigned a horrified expression. "A ghost? Down in the lobby?"

"One with icy blue eyes and dark hair."

"Ah...so we're speaking of Kent."

"No, we're not, other than in the past tense." Her tone of voice had an edge to it she couldn't hide.

"I heard you two had started seeing each other," Arnie said carefully.

"From Kent?"

"He hinted at it, last time I talked to him. That was a few weeks ago." Arnie lifted his eyebrows in a patient expression. "We're not quite on friendly terms just now."

Nellie was surprised. "Why?"

"We have different philosophies about things," he replied vaguely. "So, I take it you're on the outs with him, too?"

"Yes. I've doused and buried the torch I carried for him all last year."

Arnie's eyes brightened. "You're serious?"

"Morbidly serious," she said in a flat tone. "All it took was a few actual dates with him and it fizzled. Mostly my fault," she added, bowing her head. "But it's for the best. I see now that he wasn't right for me. I'd made a fantasy out of him that wasn't based on anything real. It was dumb of me to be so crazy about him."

Arnie's eyes were still glowing as he studied her. "Interested in having lunch? You can tell me about what happened, if you like. Talking can be therapeutic. Besides, I played a part in your campaign to romance him. I'm curious as to what went wrong."

Nellie had spent the weekend all by herself stewing about her breakup with Kent. Despite her positive resolutions to get over the event, she thought Arnie's offer to talk it over might help her get past the feeling of loss that still seemed to cling to her soul. And besides, she'd vowed to go out with the first decent man who asked her, and Arnie filled the bill.

"That sounds nice," she said, injecting some enthusiasm into her tone of voice. "I'll try not to be maudlin. You have to promise not to repeat any of our conversation to him, though."

"Promise," Arnie said with a nod of his head. "I've begun not to think of him as a close friend anymore. I haven't even seen him since he moved to Worldwide. So it won't be a hard promise to keep."

Nellie felt sad that Arnie's friendship with Kent seemed to be dissolving. "That's too bad. You and he were pretty close, weren't you?"

"Yeah, but people outgrow one another sometimes." He shrugged. "Shall we meet at eleven-thirty?"

At lunchtime, Arnie took her by cab to Berghoff's on Adams Street. "This is my favorite place," he told her as the white-aproned waiter handed them menus. After they'd ordered, he said, "So, let's have all the gory details."

Nellie began by telling him about the book she'd bought.

*"How To Marry Your Dreamboat?"* he repeated, laughing. "You've got to be kidding."

She felt embarrassed. "I can't believe I did that, either. Me, with a college degree and a C.P.A. certificate. It just shows how ridiculously desperate I was." She went on to explain how she'd used the information he'd given her about Kent, making up a work sheet to keep track, and the various times she'd invented interests in things to have a reason to talk to Kent and catch his attention.

"I remember the billy goat story," Arnie said with a chuckle. "I had the feeling you were up to something in that conversation. Kent seemed to buy it, though."

Nellie's shoulders rose as she drew in a long breath. "Yes," she said, sighing with guilt. "He was like a lamb being led to the slaughter. But he wound up slaughtering me."

"What happened?"

Nellie decided Arnie didn't need to know every

detail, particularly the intimate ones. "He asked me out—beginning with the Art Institute."

Arnie laughed again. "That guy is so predictable."

"And I wowed him with stuff I'd looked up in a library art book. Then I found out what store he shopped at and when, and I waited in my car so I could happen to walk in while he was there." She stopped and rubbed her forehead. "Telling you all the sneaky things I did is really embarrassing."

Arnie leaned forward and smiled. "Don't be embarrassed. You think there aren't other women out there who do things like that?"

"I'm sure there are, but I had never aspired to be one of them."

He shook his head. "We all do crazy, out-of-character things now and then. It's how we learn who we are. Besides, Kent's got his own premeditated dating methods, and unfortunately, in his case, they aren't out of character."

Nellie widened her eyes. "He does? Like what?"

Arnie shifted in his chair as if annoyed. "Like taking women to the Art Institute. You made a list—well, he had his list, too. He used a different approach, but it's all calculated to get him what he thinks he wants."

"He has a list? What kind of list?"

Arnie paused, as if thinking better of what he'd said, and then shook his head. "I probably shouldn't tell you any more. He and I are drifting apart, but it's not right for me to break his confidences. I promised you I wouldn't say anything about this conversation, and—though I can't remember ever promising Kent not to repeat things he's told me—I probably should treat his conversations with me the same way. In any case, the last time I talked to him, he claimed he'd changed. I just didn't believe it.''

Nellie was immensely curious about what Arnie knew, but she had to respect his sense of what was appropriate.

"So you saw him at the grocery store?" Arnie prompted her to continue where she'd left off.

"Yes. I even got him to take me to his place. Things grew more romantic after that. We saw a lot of each other. The relationship progressed," she said, summarizing intimate details. "And then, just when he seemed ready to propose, I got this huge feeling of guilt for having lied to him and tricked him. I showed him the book and the work sheet I'd made. I confessed everything. He was shocked, got angry, said he never wanted to speak to me again and left. That's how it ended.''

Arnie seemed speechless for a moment, as if astonished by her story. "Wait a minute. You say he was about to propose? Marriage?"

"I think so. Later on, he denied it. But I was sure he was." She tried to remember Kent's words, but couldn't quite be sure anymore exactly what he'd said. "Maybe I was mistaken, or assuming too much.''

Arnie tilted his head to one side. "Well, if you thought so, then maybe he was. I'm just…surprised. You're not what he always claimed he was looking for. Maybe he *had* changed." He seemed to ponder the thought a moment longer. "Well, anyway, my other question is—why the hell did you tell him? If you'd kept quiet, you might have been engaged to him now.''

Unexpected tears stung her eyes. She thought she'd gotten past her histrionics. Blinking back the moisture, she said with self-deprecation, ''You think that didn't occur to me, even before I told him? How could I let a man marry me, when I'd been so dishonest toward him? I felt that I had to clear that up, and I guess I'd just hoped he'd try to understand and forgive me. It had seemed so harmless in the beginning—a white lie here, a little fib there. And it had worked—and kept on working. Pretty soon I'd created this whole web of falsehoods about myself so he would like me. And he did. If I'd have married him, he'd have figured out eventually that I wasn't on his wavelength the way I pretended to be.''

Arnie smiled at her with a sort of sad admiration. ''It's ironic. In confessing your dishonesty, you've proved yourself to be more honest than most. Too bad Kent couldn't see that.''

Tears filled her eyes again and streamed down her cheeks before she could stop them. To have someone praise her when she'd felt so ashamed touched her deeply. ''Thanks,'' she whispered, drying her eyes with her napkin. ''Sorry. Didn't mean to get all emotional.'' She tried to laugh. ''I promised you I wouldn't be maudlin.''

''That's okay,'' Arnie said. ''You...you think you'll be able to get over him?''

Nellie sniffed and made an effort to compose herself. ''Of course.'' She tried to speak with confidence. ''When I saw him in the lobby, I walked right by him and didn't flinch. I'm over him.''

Arnie shook his head. "I don't think so."

"Well, if I'm not over him, then I intend to get over him—fast," she insisted. "I'm ready and eager to date other men. I'm very happy to be having lunch with you. I'm having a nice time."

Arnie smiled. "I'm glad. We can do this again later in the week, if you like."

"I'd love it. Anytime."

"How about a regular date? Like dinner and a movie? You'd go out with me?"

"Absolutely!"

Arnie stared at her as if he didn't quite believe her.

"What?" she asked, wondering why he was studying her so doubtfully.

"I have the feeling that it'll be like dating a widow who hasn't gotten over her dead husband yet."

After lunch, they walked out onto Adams Street. The sun had come out and the temperature had risen. Suddenly it had turned into one of those sparkling, pleasant winter days that helped Chicagoans forget the bad days.

"Want to walk back to the office instead of hailing a cab?" Arnie asked. "It's so nice out."

She readily agreed, and they decided to take the most scenic route, up Michigan Avenue. When they passed the Art Institute, Nellie kept her eyes ahead, focusing on the tall, black, John Hancock building in the distance.

They made small talk along the way. As they crossed Randolph Street on the way to their office building, all at once Arnie nudged her arm.

"Speak of the devil," he said, using his eyes to

direct her attention to a man approaching the opposite corner of Randolph and Michigan. He was carrying a briefcase and looking at his watch.

"Oh, my God." Nellie's heart seemed to stop as she saw Kent. Unlike this morning in the lobby, it would be hard to avoid speaking with him, since she was with Arnie. While they could simply ignore each another on their own, Kent and Arnie would no doubt feel required to at least say hello.

"Don't panic," Arnie quietly told her.

"Isn't there some way we can avoid him? Turn around and go back across the street?" She knew it was a childish idea, but she had the strong desire to turn and run from the situation.

"He's already seen us," Arnie said as they stepped up from the street onto the sidewalk.

Indeed, Kent was about thirty feet away, and he was staring at the couple, his blue eyes full of shock.

"Hey, Kent!" Arnie said as the distance between them closed. Nellie tried to hang back, but Arnie took her by the elbow and made her keep up with his pace. "On your way to a client?"

"Yeah. In the Prudential building." Kent eyed the two of them. Nellie lowered her eyes and wet her lips. "Haven't seen you for a while," he said to Arnie.

"No. I'd like to get a look at your new office one of these days."

"Sure. Come up anytime," Kent replied tensely.

No one spoke for a lengthy moment.

"You remember Nellie," Arnie said, laying his hand on her shoulder.

"Yes." Kent eyed Nellie grimly, then turned his darkening eyes back to Arnie. "Out for lunch?"

"Right," Arnie replied. "Gorgeous day, huh?"

"What's going on?" he asked Arnie in a quiet but sharp tone.

"Going on?"

"Are you two an item, now?"

"We only had lunch," Arnie replied.

Nellie looked askance.

"You don't know what you're getting into," Kent warned him, then turned his eyes on Nellie.

She felt his stare and she looked up. When she saw the anger in his eyes, she grew determined not to be intimidated and glared back at him.

"It sure didn't take you long to forget Saturday night," Kent said in a deceptively easy tone.

"I haven't forgotten," she told him, raising her chin. "I thought you were never going to speak to me again."

Kent seemed startled at having his own vow thrown back at him. "You're right," he said with a firm nod of his head. "I wasn't." He turned to Arnie and said in a mock-friendly tone, "Careful. You may be in over your head."

"So you two have broken up," Arnie said, as if he hadn't been sure. "I figured it was only a matter of time. Too bad. Just because you didn't appreciate her, doesn't mean I can't."

"*Appreciate* her?" Kent repeated the word with disdain. "I don't even know who she is anymore. And neither do you!"

"Don't make ignorant assumptions," Arnie replied, his tone amused and a bit smug.

Nellie looked back and forth between them, growing more and more perturbed. "Do you two have to talk about me as if I weren't standing here?"

Kent gave her a withering stare. "As far as I'm concerned, you're *not* here."

His remark devastated her even more than the things he'd said Saturday night. He'd been in shock then and could be forgiven. But he'd had time to recover, as she had. If this was his attitude toward her after having the weekend to reflect on what had happened, then she couldn't forgive him for saying that, to him, she was a nonperson.

Wounded to the core, shaking inside, she said, "I didn't know you could be this cruel. I guess I never had a clue who you really are, either."

Kent's eyes widened and he seemed slightly off balance. But he stepped sideways, quickly covering his reaction, his expression growing set and grim.

Arnie, who'd been listening to their repartee with interest, said, "Boy, I'm in treacherous territory here!"

"Yes, this is what we've been reduced to," Kent said, staring at Nellie accusingly. The deep hurt reappeared in his cold eyes.

"I know it's my fault. I apologized—profusely," she told Kent. "I thought you might at least *try* to understand. I thought you were kind and forgiving. Silly me. I suppose you've never done anything you're ashamed of. I suppose it would be lowering your standards of perfection to even tolerate a woman who could make a mistake. Maybe you'll find some paragon of virtue somewhere, and then you'll be equally matched."

"I make mistakes, too," Kent said, losing his cool

countenance, his voice sardonic. "I thought I was fairly sophisticated, but I believed *you* were perfect. You led me to think you were. I hadn't realized I harbored that old-fashioned ideal about finding a woman who was pure, sweet and honest. Actually you did me a favor. You burst that bubble with a great big pin, and now I'm back in the gritty real world again. Only wiser and educated by the school of hard knocks."

"I wish I had a violin," Arnie said in an arch, dramatic way. "This speech should be accompanied by music."

Nellie gave Arnie an annoyed look. She didn't appreciate his amusement at such a tense moment.

Kent glared at Arnie with impatience. "Grow up."

"I was just going to say that to you," Arnie retorted.

Kent grew exasperated. "God, why am I standing here talking to you two?"

"Because there's obviously unfinished business between the two of *you*," Arnie said, pointing to him and then Nellie. "If it takes me being here, impertinent comments and all, to get you two to hash it out, then I'll do it."

"Why the self-sacrifice?" Kent asked suspiciously.

"Because," Arnie explained, "once your unfinished business is finished, however it settles out, then all three of us can move on. I think you can read between the lines."

Kent's eyes and stern jaw carried such a mixture of emotion—anger, hurt, jealousy—that Nellie thought he might burst. "Consider it settled," he told Arnie.

Arnie took a long breath and let it out slowly. "I don't think so," he said, looking at his friend with curious sympathy. "You're a mess."

"You're nuts," Kent replied. "I'm late for my appointment." He began to walk on down the sidewalk.

"Anytime you want to talk—" Arnie offered.

"Not anytime soon," Kent said dourly over his shoulder. His eyes settled for a moment on Nellie.

She looked back at him, upset and nervous from the confrontation. "Goodbye," she said softly, not sure if she should say anything to him under the circumstances.

He seemed taken off guard again and, as if shamed by her politeness, he lowered his eyes and said, "Goodbye." She thought she heard a hint of tenderness in his voice as he said the word. But as he walked briskly down the street, away from them, she decided she must have been mistaken.

"He's carrying a heavy load," Arnie commented as he and Nellie turned to continue toward their office building.

"His briefcase?" she said, trying to be blithe and sarcastic.

"No. I think he's still in love. He's got a long row to hoe to get over you."

"You heard the things he said to me," Nellie argued, not believing Arnie's interpretation. "He was so hateful."

"Exactly. Completely out of character for Kent. He may be ambitious, but he's always been a gentleman—never hurts anyone's feelings on purpose. I've seen him angry about things that have gone wrong at the office over the years. He gets stern, but he never chews anybody out. He always listens to the other point of view. But with you—suddenly he's Scrooge. He's in love and been hurt. Probably never happened to him before. He doesn't know how to react, except to build up his fortifications so he won't be hurt again.''

Nellie thought over what Arnie had said. Arnie might be right—he'd been Kent's best friend for years. ''So, if that's his reaction, there's no hope he'll forgive me.''

''You still want him to forgive you?''

''I'd like to be on good terms with him,'' she replied. ''I certainly don't expect to ever marry him. I wouldn't want to, now.'' She said this with conviction.

''Really? Honest?'' Arnie said, looking at her with a wary smile. ''Now don't fib to *me*. I have feelings, too.''

Nellie chewed her lip. Growing discouraged now, doubts clouding her conviction, she found she had trouble answering his question in the affirmative. ''Maybe I'm lying to myself,'' she finally said with a sigh. ''I don't want to hurt you, too.''

He nodded. ''I know. Don't worry. I don't have any rose-colored glasses on. I'm beginning to see the lay of the land.''

''The lay of the land?''

''Well, you've got the Appalachians in the East— that's you. And the Rockies in the West—that's Kent. And the Mississippi in between. Somebody's got to ford the river.''

Nellie smiled. ''And what landform are you?''

''I'm Lake Michigan. Above it all and watching

the weather patterns to see how fast erosion takes place.''

She laughed. "You're funny. Why didn't I fall in love with you?''

Arnie lifted his red eyebrows whimsically. "Beats me.''

# 7

Kent walked back to his office from the Prudential building late in the afternoon. As he passed the intersection of Randolph and Michigan, he couldn't help but be reminded of his unpleasant conversation earlier with Nellie and Arnie. He felt bad about it. He and Arnie had been such good friends. Now they were sniping at each other, and all because of Nellie. It was amazing how one pair of innocent big brown eyes could cause so much trouble between old friends.

Kent felt a surge of guilt as he remembered the pain in those brown eyes, when he'd told Nellie that as far as he was concerned, she wasn't there. She'd called him cruel. He supposed he was; but then, what she'd done to him wasn't very pretty, either. She was just one surprise after another. Out with Arnie already, after the way she'd made eager, passionate love to him, Kent! Still, he ought to try to rise above it all and not respond in such a hurtful way.

Well, he'd learned one lesson—to never let himself be guided by emotion again. Following his yearnings and adolescent ideals had almost made a fool of him. If he'd stuck to his original plan for choosing a wife, he'd never have wound up with Nellie's knife plunged into his heart.

From now on, he intended to adhere to his former, logical approach and focus on his career. It was the only sensible way to go. Never again would he lose sight of his goals. Falling in love and giving in to emotion was for chumps, for guys with no willpower who didn't know how to plan their lives. If a fellow wasn't careful, he could wind up having his whole life shifted around by one manipulative female who claimed to love him.

Quit thinking about Nellie, Kent told himself as he entered the lobby of his building. He looked around, half-afraid he'd run into her again, but she was nowhere to be seen. He hurried toward his elevator before the doors closed.

As he felt the slightly queasy effect on his stomach from the quick escalation to the higher floors of the building, he purposely turned his thoughts to Arnie. He hated to see their friendship deteriorate. He missed their old camaraderie. Arnie had a certain down-to-earth humor that Kent enjoyed. Besides, he owed it to Arnie, out of respect for their long friendship, to make him see that he was in dangerous territory dating Nellie.

Kent went into his new office, took off his coat and stood in front of his window for a moment. People walking on the sidewalks below in the shadows of tall buildings looked small and insignificant. The view seemed to help put things into perspective for Kent. Life was too short and precarious to stay angry, especially with your best friend.

He picked up the phone and dialed Arnie's extension. It rang once and then he heard a male voice.

"Arnie Hammersmith. Can I help you?"

"It's Kent."

There was a slight pause on the other end of the line. "Kent. Thought you weren't going to talk to me anytime soon."

It was the second time that day that Kent had had a statement of his thrown back at him. At least it was less unsettling coming from Arnie.

"I shouldn't have said that," Kent apologized. "I...was aggravated by the...that whole conversation on the street. Let's forget it. I have. You said you'd like to see my new office."

"Sure. When?"

"I'll be here for the rest of the afternoon, cleaning up odds and ends. You can come by whenever you want. Or tomorrow if you prefer."

"No, today's good. I just have another hour of work on my computer. See you then."

"Great." Kent hung up, feeling relieved.

An hour later, Kent looked up to find Arnie at his door.

"Hey, nice view!" Arnie said, coming in to look out the window. "You can even see a patch of the lake."

"Grant Park, too," Kent said, pointing.

"Impressive. So, how's the atmosphere up here?"

Kent smiled. "The people are fine. The air temperature seems to be either too hot or too cold, though."

"They make good coffee in Worldwide?"

"Tolerable. Like some?"

"Not now, thanks."

Kent motioned toward a small upholstered chair in front of his desk. "Sit down."

Arnie seated himself. "They're talking about giving me a corner office, now that I'm a manager, too. Just talk so far, though."

"They'll come through. Complain if they don't."

There was an awkward silence then.

Arnie broke it. "So, you've forgotten all about the conversation on the street this afternoon?"

"Yup."

"Really?" Arnie persisted. "See, I find that hard to believe."

Kent shifted uneasily in his chair. "I'm sorry I was testy with you. Let's just forget it happened."

Arnie shook his head. "That's not how the human mind works. You don't forget an emotional confrontation until you make peace with it and move on."

"Are you turning into a therapist now?"

"Psychology was my minor in college, and don't try to evade the issue."

"Okay, I won't," Kent agreed. "But since you won't let it go, I suspect it's your issue, too. You're dating Nellie, aren't you?"

"We've only had lunch together. We haven't had a real date yet—though she said she'd go out with me."

Kent seized the opportunity to warn his friend again. "I told you, you may be in over your head with that girl."

"Over my head? Nellie's not tall enough."

Kent ignored Arnie's quip. "She's not as sweet and innocent as she appears. She went after me with a carefully organized scheme—read a book about how to catch a husband, made up a work sheet listing all my favorite things and—''

"I gave her some of that information," Arnie interrupted, as if not needing to hear the details.

"I know," Kent said with asperity. "She told me."

Arnie did not look the least bit embarrassed.

"Vying for the Benedict Arnold award?" Kent needled him.

"I'm a big traitor because I told her you like jazz and played the sax? She's my friend, too, and she was desperate to get you to notice her before you moved up to this floor. I agreed to tell her some innocuous facts about you. So string me up by my thumbs!"

"You *willingly* gave her ammunition to get my attention?''

"I didn't think it would work," Arnie said, shrugging his shoulders. "You were so dead-set on marrying a certain type of woman, I figured you wouldn't bother with Nellie, even if she did strike up conversations about your favorite topics. I thought she'd give up on you and move on to other men—like me, for instance. You always denied you had any attraction to her. How was I to know that you would rush into her conspicuous snare?"

"I admit I walked straight into it without a clue," Kent said ruefully. "I thought she was this innocent little thing who was incapable of schemes and deceptions. She lied to me, Arnie."

"And how do you know she lied?"

"Because she told me. She admitted it—showed

me the damn book and her elaborate work sheet. I felt like such a fool!''

"Well," Arnie calmly said, straightening up in his chair, "I have to tell you, I'd be damned flattered if any woman went to such lengths to win *me*."

"Maybe you should prepare yourself to be 'flattered' then," Kent said, pointing at him. "How do you know that she's not scheming now to marry you?"

"I wish," Arnie stated with weary irony. "And as far as Nellie's scheming goes, weren't you just as calculating when you came up with your list of prerequisites to find the 'right' wife? When you take women to the Art Institute, is it because you're an art lover, or is it because you want to impress them by pretending to be a classy guy? Is that so different than what Nellie did?"

Kent bristled as Arnie's point hit home. "Okay, but I merely had a general plan. Nellie went so far as to do detective work on me. I'm convinced she even hung out by the grocery store where I shop, so she could meet me there by 'accident.' The woman is treacherous."

"If she's so treacherous, then why did she confess everything to you?"

"Couldn't live with her guilt, I suppose," Kent said, feeling that was beside the point. "The thing is, she's capable of lies and deceit."

"But she can't seem to maintain the deceit—she confessed. She may have lost her sense of right and wrong for a short time, but she's so innately honest, she had to rectify the situation. Seems to me that she's a lot more honest than the average person."

Kent got up and paced the length of his office. He turned to Arnie. "Okay, she did the right thing. She begged me to forgive her." He pressed his lips together for a moment as he clenched his jaw. "And maybe I should forgive her, just to do the altruistic thing. But that doesn't mean I'm ever going to be stupid enough to get involved with her again."

"Maybe she doesn't want to get involved with *you* again," Arnie said, pulling on his earlobe. "On the street corner this afternoon she said you were cruel and that she'd never known who you really were. Sounds like she's decided you're not the man she thought she loved. So, relax. I think you're safe from being bothered by her anymore," he finished blithely.

Kent now felt about two inches tall. "Well, then it's all working out the way it should," he said, trying to copy Arnie's breezy attitude. "She doesn't want me anymore, and I don't want her." His tone grew tense despite his intention to make light of the situation. "And that leaves you free to pick up the pieces."

Arnie rose from his chair. "Yeah, lucky me. Now that we've got that settled, I'll leave you to contemplate in your new office your happy prospects for the future. You've almost got it all, Kent. All you need is that perfect corporate wife. Hope you find her!" With that, Arnie saluted Kent and walked out the door.

Kent sat down behind his desk and massaged his forehead. Arnie had given him a headache. He glanced at the spreadsheets on his desk that he'd been going over when Arnie came in. The columns of numbers blurred and he decided he couldn't get any more work done tonight. He locked his briefcase in a file drawer, grabbed his coat and left.

When he walked out of the building, the temperature was still mild and the sky clear. There wasn't even much wind, which was unusual for the Windy City. He decided, since the weather was so pleasant, that he'd walk the couple of miles home instead of using public transportation. A long walk might do him good.

He headed up Michigan Avenue toward the bridge over the Chicago River. As he walked, he pondered Arnie's comment about how Kent almost had it all. Despite his recent promotion, he felt pretty empty. He'd gotten into uncharted territory following his heart with Nellie and he was still finding his way back to the main road. He'd better stick to his grand plan for his life—it was the safest way to go.

He was reminded of Arnie's comment that his plan was just as calculated as Nellie's scheme. Kent still didn't entirely agree, but he had to admit to himself that Arnie had a point. He'd invented a personal formula for success, and she had invented a way to grasp at love. Where would they be now, he found himself wondering, if neither of them had ever formed a plan, but had just let nature take its course? They probably would have fallen in love on the candy factory audit and might be married by now.

The thought shook him, and made him even more pensive. He was brooding by the time he started across the Michigan Avenue bridge. He glanced to his right at the slow-moving river and the lake beyond. As he faced forward again, he caught sight of a woman at the far end of the bridge who had paused by the railing and was staring down at the water below. Her stature was short and he recognized her long brown hair and gray coat.

Kent slowed his pace, thinking twice about whether he should try to avoid Nellie. As he studied her profile, he sensed a sadness in her posture and bleak gaze. She was brooding at least as much as he was, he realized. Perhaps she was still hurting from the comment he'd made on the street corner.

Maybe he ought to take this opportunity to apologize to her. Kent was glad to be on good terms again with Arnie. He might feel even better if he were at least civil to Nellie, instead of leaving his angry words hanging between them. A simple apology didn't mean he had any intention of rekindling their romance, and she was smart enough to understand that. Admitting he'd been insensitive could do no harm, and it might even help him move on toward his goal with no baggage weighing him down.

Kent picked up his pace again, crossing the bridge with a sense of purpose. But when he was about twenty feet from Nellie, she suddenly wiped her eyes with her hand and then turned and started walking. She hadn't seen Kent; he was fairly certain. She still seemed lost in her own thoughts, thoughts that had apparently brought her to tears.

As he followed her to the end of the bridge, he noted her graceful stride, her hair billowing behind her. He remembered the Saturday he'd walked beside her on their way to his condo, how masculine her feminine presence had made him feel, how strong and sublime the natural chemistry between them had been. He sensed that chemistry was still there, waiting to be tapped. If he caught up with her now and walked beside her, he'd probably feel the same way in a matter of seconds.

Kent began to wonder if he should close the distance between them and apologize as he'd intended. He quickly decided not to, for several reasons. He could see she was upset, for one thing. He didn't want to chance distressing her more. Nor did he want to risk feeling sorry for her. He might be drawn into comforting her and wind up in dangerous emotional territory again. Just walking up the street with her might remind them both of what they'd found and lost in each other.

No, it would be best to make amends to her when both were less vulnerable than they were now. Perhaps a few weeks from now, and at the office in a more businesslike atmosphere—not on a beautiful day outdoors when the wind was blowing through her hair, making her look glowing and sensual. Kent didn't want to tempt his powers of resistance—he might not have any.

He slowed his pace until he was about forty feet behind her. They passed the old Water Tower. When she came to Water Tower Place she stopped and looked at some women's suits in the display window at Marshall Field's. After about half a minute, she walked into the shopping center. Kent stayed on his path up North Michigan Avenue, relieved that she had apparently decided to shop.

By the time he was a few blocks from his condo, he found himself wondering exactly why she'd been staring at the river in tears. Had she really been crying over him, or was he being egotistical to assume so?

If he *was* the reason, then he couldn't help but contemplate how much she must really love him. Maybe Arnie was right, maybe he should be flattered that she'd gone to such lengths to attract him.

But he'd refused to forgive her and she'd called him cruel. Maybe she wouldn't want him anymore, as Arnie had predicted. Despite Kent's renewed vow to stick to his life plan, he kept wondering about Nellie. How would she react if he did try to rekindle their relationship? *Should* she be in his future?

The following weekend, Kent attended a retirement party given for his father by the bank for which his dad had worked for so many years. Kent's mother, Barbara, was there in her best pink suit, her brown hair specially coiffed by her hairdresser for the occasion. She sat next to Jim, her gray-haired husband, quietly beaming. After the dinner, various toasts were given, including one by Kent, who proudly acknowledged the positive influence his dad had had on his life, the stable, loving home he'd provided his family.

After all the memories had been shared and Jim's accomplishments in the community recited, Jim got up to make a short speech. He thanked everyone, especially Kent, made a few jokes of his own and talked about his retirement plans. Soon his voice began to grow emotional. Kent wasn't used to seeing his dad close to tears, and he grew concerned.

"I'd like to make a toast of my own to my wife, Barbara," he said, raising his glass. "She's been patient all these years with my foibles and idiosyncrasies. I'm not the most demonstrative of husbands. Kent may have spoken in glowing terms about me, but Barbara played the larger role in raising him and instilling in him the human values we tend to forget about in the business world. My wife has always been happy to stay in the background, but she's always been at the forefront of my life. She's genuine, warm, wise and she loves unconditionally.

"I'll tell you a secret. Almost fifteen years ago, I was offered a promotion. I was flattered, but the promotion would have required me to leave the branch office where I was enjoying being a manager and move to corporate headquarters in the Loop. There, I knew I'd be caught up in the competitive corporate world, working late and on weekends to get ahead. I was also aware of the old Peter Principle—'A person rises to his level of incompetence.'"

The audience laughed.

"I didn't want that to happen to me, and I didn't want to be pulled away from my family life by a career in the competitive corporate banking world. So I declined the promotion—which is pretty unheard of. But I believed in planning my life for happiness, not wealth and prestige. Without Barbara, my life would never have been complete. I'm very happy that now I'll have all the time I want to spend with the woman who made my life worthwhile. To Barbara."

Kent raised his glass of champagne to his teary-eyed mother, but when he tried to drink, he found his throat too constricted with emotion to swallow. While his father made his final thank-you to those present, Kent worked to compose himself.

It was difficult, because he found himself in shock. All these years he'd thought his father had made a career miscalculation when he'd married a wife who was too shy to be an effective business asset. He'd never known his dad had declined a promotion so he wouldn't have to give up time with his wife and son. His heartfelt tribute kept repeating in Kent's mind, *Without Barbara, my life would never have been complete.* Kent never realized his dad felt that way. Like many men of the older generation, his father usually hid his feelings, and he wasn't the type to go out of his way to show affection.

Perhaps reflecting on his retirement had caused him to use this occasion to celebrate his life and his marriage. He wasn't even hesitant to proclaim in front of a large group of people his profound satisfaction with the life choices he'd made. To Kent, it was all a bit astonishing. He'd always been aware of his mother's caring personality, but tonight had revealed a private, previously unseen aspect in his father's character. He'd been more than a respected bank manager and community leader—he'd also been a man totally in love with one woman for over thirty years.

When the dinner was over, Kent hugged both his parents and told them he loved and admired them both. As he drove home to his condo, he found himself reassessing his own priorities. His father's notion of planning his life for happiness, not wealth or prestige, dominated his thoughts. It didn't take long for Kent to realize he'd been planning to make a major mistake his father had *not* made—he'd been about to pass up the opportunity to marry for love, to have a happy home life. It was becoming heartbreakingly clear to Kent that Nellie was the only "right" wife for him.

But if he proposed, would she accept? Not likely,

after the way he'd spoken to her and refused to forgive her. He'd be lucky if she'd be willing to even speak to him. Compared to Kent, Arnie probably looked to her like the proverbial knight in shining armor. Kent's heart sank. He hoped he hadn't ruined his own chance at marrying the one woman who could make his life complete. Maybe she'd lied to him, but it was because she was grasping at happiness, too. At least she had a better sense of what true happiness was than Kent had.

God, what if he'd stuck to his plan and married some golden girl just because she was blond and vivacious? What a shallow marriage it might have been. What a shallow life he would have had, focused on business and getting ahead. When it came time for Kent to retire decades from now, would he have been able to say what his dad had said?

Nellie had tugged at his heart the day he first met her. She possessed many of his mother's qualities—it was no wonder he'd felt so at home with her so quickly. She'd kept on trying to tug at him, but he hadn't let her. He'd insisted to himself over and over that she wasn't the woman he wanted.

If it had taken her crazy scheme to get him to realize he loved her, why should he hold that against her? She'd awakened him, made him see what life was really about. Perhaps, years ago, his mom had that very same effect on his dad. Maybe his dad had been quicker than Kent had been at realizing that true love was something to value, not to push aside.

Had he pushed Nellie aside once too often, and in too harsh a way? Could she ever accept him back into her life? The tables had been turned. Now it was Kent who needed to figure out some method to win Nellie.

# 8

Nellie walked to her office building Monday morning pulling up the wool scarf around her neck to just below her ears, trying to close the gap of bare skin beneath her knit cap. A neck bared to the shivery winter wind was a consequence she hadn't foreseen when she'd gotten her hair cut.

It had been an impetuous whim. Late last week she'd seen her sister's latest commercial on TV for the first time. Jeannie had mentioned on the phone that she'd gotten a new haircut, and Nellie thought she looked absolutely beautiful in the commercial for a famous brand-name athletic shoe. Her medium-length brown hair bobbed exquisitely in the slow motion shots of her running through Central Park.

Nellie had been wondering for quite a while whether she shouldn't get a shorter haircut. With her five-foot-three-inch stature, youthful face and long hair, she apparently looked too much like a young girl to some of her clients. One client had been doubtful enough that she was who she claimed she was, he'd called Latham & Eliot to verify that she was indeed the C.P.A. assigned to their audit. A shorter, more businesslike haircut might help solve that problem.

There was another reason that she felt she needed a change. She'd been depressed all last week after her encounter with Kent on the street corner. Though she kept up an appearance of equanimity at the office, when she went home, she often found herself near tears.

The very evening of that incident she'd stopped on the Michigan Avenue bridge for a long while, blankly staring at the water flowing below. The fact that Kent considered her a nonperson had sunk in even deeper by then than in their afternoon confrontation. She couldn't remember ever feeling so low in her life. She'd tried to perk herself up by shopping at Marshall Field's, but it hadn't worked. After about fifteen minutes of drifting among clothes racks, she'd left without buying anything and gone home.

She'd recalled her vows to forget Kent, discover herself, and be proud of who she was. And then she'd seen her sister on TV and decided that maybe a new look would be good for her, too. She'd made an appointment for a haircut on Saturday afternoon.

Tammy, her thirtyish, blond hairstylist, had started by cutting her hair to a medium length, as Nellie had requested. She'd blown it dry for Nellie and styled it.

As she'd stared at herself in the mirror, she'd hesitantly told Tammy, "It's nice. I do look more businesslike."

Tammy had smiled knowingly. "But you're not quite happy with it."

"It doesn't look...different enough. I wanted to look like a whole new person, you know?"

"Have you just broken up with a boyfriend?" Tammy had asked.

The question had startled Nellie. "Well, yes. Why?"

"It's the Mia Farrow syndrome," Tammy had said. "That's what the older stylists always say. Years ago, when Mia Farrow broke up with Frank Sinatra, she got her hair cut super short. She did it to show her independence and a new attitude."

Nellie had smiled. "So I'm not the first woman to go through this process."

"Not by a long shot. But it seems to have a therapeutic effect. If you want it shorter, I'll cut it that way." Tammy had used her comb to lift some of the hair above Nellie's forehead. "We can leave it longer on top so it still looks feminine, and wispy sideburns by your ears would be pretty. Brunettes usually look good with short cuts. Want to go for it?"

"Go for it!" Nellie had replied, settling back in her chair to start the haircut process all over again.

Tammy hadn't hedged her bets. When she'd finished, there was more of Nellie's hair on the floor than on her head. When she'd looked at her finished new do in the mirror, she had a mixture of feelings—panic and emancipation. She'd gotten her wish. Nellie looked like a whole new person.

After struggling with her scarf, she was happy to enter the warm lobby of her building and get out of the wind. She pulled off her cap and ran her fingers through her short hair to fluff it back into shape as she headed toward the elevator. Someone brushed past her in a hurry, knocked her elbow, and the cap slipped out of her hand. She stooped to pick it up.

A male voice said, "Sorry. I'll get it."

Both their hands took hold of the hat at the same time. As she looked up to say thank-you, her mouth opened, but no words came out. It was Kent.

His blue eyes were almost round with surprise. He let go of the cap and they stood, facing each other in mutual shock. Nellie quickly collected herself, mumbled thanks and resumed walking to the elevator.

Kent took hold of her arm and kept her from moving. "Wait." He stared at her for a long, puzzled moment. "You cut your hair!"

"No kidding. Very observant."

"W-why?"

As if she was going to stand there and explain to *him* her reasons! "I felt like it."

"Okay," he said agreeably, as if sensing that he was antagonizing her. "I'll get used to it. I like it already."

Was she supposed to care what he thought? Why was he bothering with her? Why didn't he just move on to his elevator? "You *approve*," she said sarcastically. "What a relief! Now I can make it through the day." She jerked her elbow out of his grasp and headed toward her elevator.

"Wait," he said, hurrying after her. "I wanted to talk to you. I'm glad we ran into each other."

She slowed her pace and looked at him as he caught up with her. "Talk to me? What is there left to say to each other at this point? In your mind I don't exist!"

"I'm sorry about that remark," he told her, looking quite earnest. "It *was* cruel. I apologized to Arnie and

I wanted especially to apologize to you for my attitude. I was angry and unkind that day."

Nellie drew in a breath and pursed her lips as she exhaled. "Okay," she said quietly. "Apology accepted. Now we're all politely squared away with each other. Things can go back to normal." She kept moving toward the elevator, whose door was opening.

"Thanks," he said, keeping up with her fast pace. "Will you have lunch with me?"

She glared at him as if he'd gone bonkers. "*Lunch?* Look, your apology is adequate. You don't have to make amends by buying me lunch."

"No, I want to talk to you," he repeated as they approached the elevator.

Others already waiting were getting on. As she paused in line, she said, "You're talking to me *now*. We've said it all. We're finished." What was with him? she wondered.

Her turn came and she walked into the crowded elevator. There was space for only one or two more people. To her astonishment, Kent stepped in and stood next to her.

"Where are you going?" she whispered to him. "This isn't your elevator."

He narrowed his eyebrows as if not following her logic.

"Aren't you going up to Worldwide?" she asked. "You have to use the other elevator."

Light seemed to dawn in his blue eyes. "You're right!" Laughing as if embarrassed at himself, he hurried to press the button that would hold open the doors just as they began to close. "Sorry," he apologized to everyone in the elevator. As he stepped off, he said to Nellie, "Talk to you later."

Her mouth open in astonishment, she watched him walk off. As the doors closed, some of the people behind her were chuckling.

"He's sure stuck on you," a man in the back joked. "Can't even figure out where he's going!"

Nellie smiled and helplessly shook her head in confusion. The man in back was certainly wrong. Kent didn't care one iota for her. But what more did he want to talk to her about?

By the time she reached her floor and got to her desk, a possible reason had entered her mind. Perhaps he felt he needed to say that he forgave her for her underhanded way of pursuing him. The night she'd confessed, he'd said he could never forgive her. Maybe he'd decided he ought to, just to wipe the slate clean. They were employees of the same firm. He probably had decided it wasn't good business to be at enmity with anyone.

Well, she could handle that, she decided. She even had time to think about her reply.

Kent didn't phone to ask her to have lunch again, as she'd half expected him to. Maybe he'd changed his mind about talking to her. She wouldn't be surprised if he had—he was getting so unpredictable. Just as well. She really had no wish to talk to him.

At different times during the day, Arnie and Rudy both complimented her on her haircut. She had the feeling, however, that neither one of them really liked it. They were used to her as a long-haired female and didn't like the change. "Looks neat," Rudy told her, as if neatness was the most positive aspect of her new do that he could find to say anything about.

Arnie's comment was more telling. "You look... sophisticated," he said dubiously. "It's nice, but... are you sure it's you?"

"It's the new me," she told him.

"Oh." Arnie seemed to absorb her answer for a moment. "Well, that's great, but I liked the old you, too."

She smiled and said thank-you.

The women on the floor weren't so ambivalent. "You look terrific, Nellie!" and "Wow, what a beautiful cut. Who's your stylist?" were two typical comments from her female co-workers. By the end of the day, as she cleaned off her desk for the evening, she was feeling darned good about herself.

And then she looked up to see Kent approaching her desk. Her heart started beating in a slow panic. She'd thought he'd forgotten. Quickly she calmed herself and pulled her mind together to deal with him.

"Hi," he said, smiling, his heavy wool coat over his arm. "I got sidetracked today with a new client. Are you free for dinner?"

Nellie leaned back in her chair, keeping her composure. "Kent, I appreciate your going out of your way to make amends with me, but you needn't feel you have to take me to lunch or dinner. I'm planning to go straight home tonight."

He lowered his eyes, looking disappointed. "I thought we could talk—"

"The office is almost empty. Pull over a chair and say what you have to say now."

He nodded, laid his coat on a nearby desk and

pulled over the chair behind the desk. When he sat down, facing her, the earnest expression she'd seen earlier returned to his face.

"That night when I was at your place, you asked me to forgive you and I said I couldn't. I want you to know that I've reconsidered. I do forgive you."

So she'd been correct, she thought, relaxing a bit. He just wanted to wipe the slate clean. "Thank you," she said. "But you had a right to be angry—what I did was wrong."

"I'm not angry at all anymore," he hastened to tell her. "I think we should look upon that incident as our first fight. Now it's over and we've made up. We can resume our relationship."

She stared at him, feeling a little numb. "W-what?"

"Let's go back to that night when we made love and pretend that you never confessed and I never got angry. We were doing just great until then. Let's pick up where we left off, before everything went temporarily wrong."

Nellie felt as if she'd gone into shock. "I can't believe you're saying this. What relationship is there to resume? It was all a sham. That's what I confessed to you. What happened *did* happen, Kent. We can't pretend that you and I haven't seen hidden sides in each other's personalities that we don't like."

"I like everything about you," he said, looking confused, as if he didn't understand her argument. "You only did what you felt you had to do at the time. Sure, when you told me it came as a blow. But now I can't help but think you were pretty clever—*and*," he said with emphasis, "your scheme worked and we got romantically involved. It bothers me to think that I might have passed you by if you hadn't done what you had.''

Nellie studied him doubtfully. ''You actually believe now that it was okay for me to lie to you the way I did?'' How could he have done such a one hundred and eighty degree turnaround in so short a time?

''Not okay,'' he said, gently. ''You made a mistake. But it was a harmless one, you're sorry about it, and you were honest enough to confess what you did.'' A new light came into his eyes, as if he'd suddenly had a moment of insight. ''I think I see why you're so resistant—you still feel guilty.''

Nellie lowered her gaze. Sure, she did, but that wasn't the entire reason she had a hard time buying into the notion that they should resume their disastrous romance.

''Look,'' he continued with renewed energy, ''let *me* make a confession. You kept a list on me—well, I used to have my own list—traits I thought the ideal woman should have. I was looking for the perfect corporate wife—blond, vivacious and classy. I was going to plan my career and my life in an ultralogical way. I was afraid my emotions might lead me off my chosen track. So you see, I was busy making life mistakes before you even thought of making yours. I had no right to be angry at you for having a scheme to get what you wanted for your life. I had one, too.''

Nellie nodded, interested in what he'd told her. She remembered Arnie saying that Kent had his own list. Now she knew what it was. However, his confession only confirmed her own convictions. ''But my scheme was to win *you*. Your scheme didn't include *me* at all. I'm not anything like the type of woman you wanted. And, I've come to realize now, you're not what I really want. So, see? It's all for the best. We're clearly not right for each other.''

His expression had grown increasingly alarmed as he listened to her. ''No, Nellie. I realized I was on the wrong track when I started seeing you. You made me forget all about my list. For the first time, my feelings *were* involved. I wasn't thinking of a woman as a business acquisition. I thought of you as the woman I loved.''

She shook her head vehemently. ''But, Kent, that's the point. You didn't love *me*. You only fell for me when I pretended to be someone else, someone who shared your every interest. On the street corner the other day, you told me you didn't know who I was. Well, you were right about that. You don't know the real me. You never did. You never loved me for myself.''

''I was drawn to you the first day I met you, Nellie. I was denying our mutual attraction the whole time we worked together at the candy factory, because I was stupidly trying to stick to my plan. I've never gotten you out of my mind. Remember when we made love?'' he said, leaning forward and lowering his voice, to make sure no one who might still be on the floor could overhear. ''Doesn't that prove we were meant to be together? What we experienced together was tangible and real.''

She wrapped her arms around her waist, feeling physical pain at that beautiful memory. ''Don't talk about that. I don't want to be reminded.''

"But we were so compatible," he argued. "It proved that our growing relationship was true and deep."

"One roll in the hay doesn't make a relationship," she told him coolly. "I don't believe you really know *what* you feel, Kent. Think about it—when we met, you liked me; then you ignored me for months, then you said you loved me after we slept together, then when I told you the truth, you hated me. Now all of a sudden, you're talking to me about love again. You can't seem to make up your mind!"

He bowed his head and rubbed his forehead. "I can see why you would doubt me. I have been mixed up about my feelings—and you haven't." He looked up at her, his eyes a deep blue. "All I can say is that I know what I want now. Everything has fallen into place in my mind. I've reexamined my priorities, and you come first."

"This week," she said dourly. "Next week you may reexamine your priorities again."

"I love you!"

"No, you don't. You fell in love with an illusion."

His ardent eyes pinned hers. "When we were in bed together, what we experienced wasn't any illusion."

"Sex is just sex," she bluntly told him.

"How would you know? You've only done it once. You have no way of knowing that what we shared doesn't always happen. You can doubt me, you can doubt we have a future together, but don't doubt what happened between us that night. That was more real than anything I've ever experienced before, and I won't let you demean it."

Nellie swallowed hard. "But what about what happened afterward?"

"That's why I'm here now, trying to get us past that. We both have made mistakes. We both have admitted them. We should forgive each other, let it go and get back to where we were when we were still lying breathless and happy in each other's arms."

Nellie felt emotion welling up inside her. She'd learned how to stand up to his anger, but she didn't know how to deal with this. "I said, don't talk about that."

"Why not? Those feelings of passion between us still exist."

"No, they don't," she said, trying to stay calm while her heart was racing inside her. She wished she could believe him, believe that they could just go back and everything would be okay, that their broken romance could still have a happy ending. But she doubted too strongly that he really loved her. He might be sincere, but he didn't know himself or her well enough to be making such absolute statements.

"Are you saying you don't feel anything toward me anymore?" he asked, his eyes demanding an answer.

"I think we've both been disillusioned with each other," she said, trying not to be hurtful.

"Yes, but I've gotten over it," he told her in no uncertain terms. "You said I'm not what you want, so obviously you're still disillusioned with me."

She wet her lips. "I don't think you love me," she repeated. "I've lost hope because our relationship was based on illusion. That's been shattered. So, yes, you can say I am disillusioned with...with everything.

Nothing can ever be the same as it was that night. We can't go back. We have to go forward.''

"Yes. Together."

"No," she said sadly, shaking her head.

"Nellie, we can't leave it this way."

"It's for the best. Let's do us both a favor and give up on each other. There's nothing to salvage. It's not going to work."

Kent straightened his back and stared at her, a new resolve forming in his eyes. "That shows you don't know *me* very well. I don't give up that easily."

"Kent—" she began to warn him.

"Going home?" he asked, changing the subject.

The question took her off guard. "Yes."

"It's a clear day. Want to walk up Michigan Avenue together?"

"I don't usually walk home," she said, finding a good reason to avoid his suggestion.

"You did last week. I saw you on the bridge."

She stared at him. "You were there?"

"Behind you. I thought about catching up with you, but...you went into Marshall Field's. You seemed a little down that night."

"We'd had that argument. You said I didn't exist."

"As if I could forget you," Kent said with a smile. "You looked so lovely with your hair blowing in the wind, the graceful way you walk. I knew getting over you would be hopeless."

"I cut my hair," she said, tugging on a lock of it. "I'm not that long-haired girl anymore. I'm not so innocent anymore. I'm not sure what you think you love, but it's changed and will never be the same."

He nodded in agreement. "You're losing a lot of

your shyness. You even look more grown-up. You're a full-fledged woman now. You're changing all right. You're getting more interesting, more beautiful and more alluring. In fact, you're a real challenge now." He smiled, his eyes full of admiration. "I love challenges."

She sighed and ran her hands through her hair in frustration. What did it take to get through to him, to get him back in touch with reality? He continued to stay on his romantic high, as if he were secretly sniffing some love potion. "Kent," she finally said, "it's time for me to go home. And I'm not walking."

"We can take the subway together."

"No."

"Share a cab?" he tried again good-naturedly.

"No. I'm taking the subway—alone. I think we've carried this conversation about as far as it can go."

"We haven't even scratched the surface," he said. "But I can see you've had enough for now. We might as well go down the elevator together—"

"I still have to put a few things away," she said. "You go. Bye."

With apparent reluctance he rose from his chair. "Okay. See you!" he said with cheerful resignation.

Her shoulders came up slightly. *See you!* was what he always used to say to her, only in a more hurried, distracted manner. She sensed it was his way of hinting that their relationship still existed. "Goodbye," she told him firmly.

He said nothing further and walked off toward the elevator.

Nellie leaned back in her chair, feeling a bit exhausted. Was he crazy? Or was she the one who was mixed up now? Did he really love her? What had made him change his mind so fast? His mercurial emotions were impossible to fathom.

When she left the building, she was afraid he might be waiting for her somewhere since he'd wanted to walk home with her. But he was nowhere to be seen. She went home and tried to get her mind off Kent by watching TV sitcoms.

But she had trouble sleeping that night. She'd managed to put their lovemaking out of her mind the last few weeks, but as she lay on her daybed, trying to fall asleep, she kept thinking of the passion she'd experienced with him there. A haunting sense of need and loss came over her, and she wished Kent had never mentioned their intimacy. She remembered the passionate way he spoke of it, of what it had meant to him, that he wouldn't let her demean that memory. But she couldn't help but feel that their lovemaking had already been demeaned by the mistakes they'd made and the angry words they'd hurled at each other. That pure unadulterated emotion they'd shared together could never be regained. Too much water had gone under the bridge—and Nellie wasn't about to jump in again.

Kent sat in the café near Nellie's apartment and asked the waitress for another order of toast and a refill on his coffee. It was Saturday. Instead of eating breakfast at home as usual, he'd gone to the café, and he'd been sitting at his table by the window for three hours, having the longest breakfast he'd ever eaten. He pretended to read a newspaper, and kept ordering food so they wouldn't ask him to leave. The place was crowded and the owners would probably have liked to have his table open up to seat those who were waiting.

He glanced out the window again. Across the street was a grocery store, a larger one than where he shopped. Nellie had mentioned that this store was one of two that she used. Since this one was closest to her apartment, he decided to stake it out first. He'd decided to use her tactic to see her outside of work. It was difficult to try to rekindle their romance at the office. The last few days, when he'd gone down to her floor after work, he'd always found she'd left early. He knew she was trying to avoid him. He'd probably come on too strong too soon, looking for a reconciliation. They were on speaking terms again, but it was clear she didn't want to be in love with him.

As the waitress poured his coffee, he glanced up to say thank-you. When he looked out the window again, he saw Nellie coming down the sidewalk on the other side of the street. She didn't even turn her head toward the café. When she reached the grocery store entrance, she pulled open the door and went in.

*Success!* Kent thought, giving himself a congratulatory thumbs-up sign. The waitress brought his toast as he was getting out his wallet. "You can have the toast," he told her. "I've got to leave now."

"So soon?" she joked, taking his credit card.

When the bill was taken care of, he left and walked across the street. It took him a while to find Nellie. She was down at the end of the far aisle in the bread section.

"Whole wheat is most healthy," he said, coming up behind her.

She turned around abruptly. "Kent! What are you doing here?"

"You checked out my grocery store. I thought I'd check out yours."

After his explanation had sunk in a moment, she glared at him. "You followed me here?"

"What's that saying about something good for the goose is good for the gander?" he replied with a grin.

"Are you trying to find a way to make fun of me?"

"Don't be so defensive," he told her. "I admit I'm using your tactic, but not to make fun of you. I'm not angry at you anymore."

Her expression cleared. "I thought you might have changed your mind again."

"No. I'm being boringly consistent. But our situations are reversed now. You're the one who's resistant, and I'm the one who has to resort to underhanded methods to get us together."

"Kent, I thought we went through all this," she said with exasperation. "Why would you want to get back together with me? We're so badly disillusioned with each other."

"Speak for yourself," he said. He glanced in her shopping cart, determined not to let her talk her way out of being in his company. "Let's see, you've got eggs, milk, sandwich meats. Which bread?"

She exhaled, grabbed a loaf of whole wheat and dropped it into the cart.

"Orange juice?" he suggested. "Need cereal?"

"I can figure out my own shopping list," she told him.

"Okay, I'll just follow along."

"Don't you have anything you need to do today?" she asked, moving down the aisle.

"Yes," he said. "Be with you."

"Kent, this isn't going to work," she told him firmly.

"Why not? It worked for you."

"But...but you didn't know what I was up to. I do. You think I'm going to let you walk home with me?"

"Yes."

"Why?"

"Because you're piling up groceries here. You're going to need some help getting them home."

"Kent, it's not going to happen—"

"I haven't seen you since the beginning of the week. You're avoiding me. Can't you give me a break? We still haven't finished the unfinished business between us."

"It's finished as far as I'm concerned," she said, grabbing an orange juice carton out of the refrigerated display case.

"Really? Nothing I said when we last talked had any impression on you?"

She looked as if she wanted to answer, but then she didn't. A subtle change in her expression, a self-consciousness in her averted eyes, told him she still had feelings that she hadn't expressed, at least not to him. It gave him hope.

He took hold of her hand. "It's time to be honest with ourselves," he said softly.

A vulnerable tenderness came across her face as he

touched her hand and held it. "I'm trying to be," she said, with difficulty.

"So am I. Let's try together. I'll help carry your groceries home and we'll talk some more, okay?"

Her delicate eyebrows drew together as if she felt some inner pain. But she said, "All right."

She picked up some other items to buy. When she'd finished, they left the store. He carried two large bags and she carried a smaller one. He began talking shop with her about Latham & Eliot, hoping to put her at ease. She kept up her part of the conversation. But as they entered her building and walked down the hall to her apartment, she grew quiet.

Kent began to feel guilty. He didn't want to impose himself on her if she really didn't want him around. It would only make her more intent on keeping her distance. "Would you rather I didn't come in?" he asked as she fumbled nervously through her purse to find her key. They were standing in front of her door.

She took out the key and looked at him. "I'd rather you didn't."

Kent felt an acute pain of disappointment. "Okay. I don't want to make a pest of myself."

She tilted her head to one side and her eyes seemed to grow moist. "I guess that's what I did with you—made a pest of myself to get you to notice me. I don't have a right to be annoyed with you for doing exactly what I did."

Kent realized he had an opportunity to take advantage of her guilt feelings, but his conscience told him not to. "You were the most precious pest I've ever had. I wish you would pester me again. The tactic doesn't seem to work very well for me. I don't seem to be charming you the way you charmed me."

Her eyes grew glassy with tears. She started to say something but then seemed to think again.

"Are you all right? I'm upsetting you, aren't I?" He set down the grocery bags by her door. "Look, I won't come in. I'll just leave these here for you to take in, and I'll go. Okay?"

As she chewed her lip, he could see her hand shaking as she held the key.

"I'm sorry, Nellie. I shouldn't have done this." He felt bad now that he'd distressed her so much. He took her lightly by the elbow and leaned down to kiss her forehead. "I'll go now."

She drew in her breath sharply as if fighting back emotion. "No, stay," she said, her voice breaking.

"You're sure you want me to?" he asked, surprised.

"I guess I don't know what I want," she told him. "Since we're trying to be honest, that's the best answer I can give." She blinked back tears and looked up at him. "You *are* charming me. You always have. Part of me says it would be better if you left, and part of me wants you to stay. Maybe I'm as confused as you."

He smiled. He knew he wasn't confused, but now wasn't the time to try to convince her of that again. "So, shall we go in?"

"Yeah," she said, sighing with what seemed to be relief, probably because she'd made a decision on her momentary dilemma. She unlocked the door as he picked up the grocery bags.

They went into the kitchen and he put the cold

items into her refrigerator while she took care of the rest. When they were finished, she asked if he wanted anything to eat or drink.

"I've been in the café across from the store, eating breakfast for three hours," he told her. "I'm stuffed."

Nellie smiled for the first time. "Three hours! Gosh, I only had to wait an hour before you showed up at your store."

"Just proves you're better at this than I am."

"Don't envy me. I have a lot of guilt to carry around because I was so successful," she said, taking off her coat.

She was wearing jeans and a flannel plaid blouse. She looked sensational, but he tried to keep his mind off her lithe figure. Much as he'd die to make love with her again, he didn't want to move too fast for her. "Don't feel guilty, Nellie," he said as he took off his own coat.

She rubbed her eyes with her fingertips. "This is such a crazy situation." When she looked up, he'd set his coat over the back of a chair by the table. Her eyes scanned his frame, seeming to pause at his shoulders and chest, and then pause again briefly at his belt or perhaps lower before she glanced away. He would have loved to jump to the conclusion that she was thinking about making love, but he decided it was dangerous to assume.

"Should we sit down in the living room and hash things out some more?" he asked.

"Yes, sure," she said, as if reminded that she was the hostess. "The living room's more comfortable."

But when they walked into the other room and saw the daybed on which they'd made love, both hesitated. Kent tried to ignore the reminder. "This room gets good sunlight during the day, doesn't it?" he said to make small talk.

"Kent, you wanted to be honest. Let's not pretend we both have forgotten that that's where we made love."

"Okay." He couldn't help but be impressed with her directness. "Let's not. It's pretty hard to pretend I don't remember every moment we spent on that little bed." He drew in a shaky breath. "How about you?"

The vulnerability he'd noticed before crept back into her eyes. "No, I haven't forgotten, either. A woman doesn't forget her first time."

"What about a second time?" Kent found himself saying this before he realized what was coming out of his mouth. He shook his head. "I didn't mean to...that's not why I'm here."

"It isn't?" Nellie's gaze met his. "It was why I wanted you to invite me up to your place." She glanced down. "Well...not to sleep with you. I was too inexperienced then to expect or want that. But I hoped that you'd...that you might kiss me." She smiled at him, looking almost as shy now as she did then. "And you did."

Kent studied her, not knowing quite how to respond, or where she was going with this new little confession. Was she only explaining and informing him of her past actions? Or was she hinting that a kiss was what she'd like to happen now? He wished he knew. He didn't want to make a mistake at this critical moment.

"I sure did," he finally said. "Couldn't help myself. You…didn't seem to mind."

"I behaved like a wanton." She looked a trifle embarrassed.

"Naturally," he said. "You were a virgin. All those pent-up desires." He felt heat rising beneath his collar. "Since we're being honest, you should know that if you see steam coming out of my ears, it's because talking about this is tapping into *my* pent-up desires. Maybe we should stop looking at and thinking about that bed and go out for a walk."

Her large brown eyes seemed to grow liquid. "You really want to…to do it again? With me?"

"Of course," he replied. "Didn't I say in our conversation by your desk that I thought we should get back to where we were when we made love? Going to bed with you again is just about all I think about."

Her eyes grew even larger. "It is?"

He felt perhaps he shouldn't be saying all this. He didn't want to scare her. On the other had, he *was* being honest. Why shouldn't she know? "Maybe you haven't been around men enough to know that we're pretty oversexed. Especially when we've found a woman who really turns us on. The worst part for me is that you've spoiled me for any other woman. You were so sweet and warm, and so responsive. Since I made love with you, I'll never be content with anyone else. Of course, that could be the best part—if we got back together. I'd be so happy that you're mine."

The soft glaze in her eyes disappeared and she seemed troubled. "Don't jump ahead, Kent. We have to figure out where we are right now. You might as well know, I feel the same. I think about being in bed with you all the time. That first experience with you was so...so life-altering and fulfilling, that when you got angry and left, I felt such a terrible loss. Like I'd discovered paradise with you and then it slipped out of my hands.''

Kent's breaths were coming faster and his heart was beginning to thud with desire and hope. ''Maybe we should make love. It was a moment of truth before. Maybe it will be again, only for the better this time. There aren't any more secrets between us, are there? Nothing more to confess to ruin everything. We're being so logical. Let's let our emotions tell us where we're at.''

Nellie's bottom lip was trembling slightly, but there was a certain light in her eyes. ''All right. I need to have that experience with you again—just to know I didn't imagine it.'' A tear rolled down her cheek. ''Even if our relationship is too scarred to survive, I want you to make love to me once more.''

He barely let her finish the sentence before he pulled her to him and kissed her, perhaps a little too aggressively. But he wanted her so much, he couldn't hold himself back. When he felt her arms slip tightly around him and her mouth clinging ardently to his, he stopped worrying and gave his emotions full rein.

She writhed against him as he ran his hands up and down her back, the heels of his hands brushing the sides of her breasts. When she turned a bit to allow his hand to caress her fully, he cupped her breast through her flannel shirt, enjoying the feel of her round, warm contours. She closed her eyes with pleasure. Kent grew so aroused he could hardly breathe, and they hadn't even taken off their clothes yet. He tried to get a grip on his desires and take it slower, for her sake. He began gently unbuttoning her shirt.

To his surprise and relief, she began helping him with the buttons. She tugged the bottom of the shirt out of the waistband of her jeans and quickly slipped it off. Underneath was a satiny pink bra. He ran his fingers over the shiny material and then upward to touch her plump flesh. She drew in a long breath, which had the effect of accentuating her cleavage.

"You're so beautiful," he murmured, sliding his hands to her shoulders to slip off the bra straps. He reached in back to unfasten the undergarment. It fell away, revealing her exquisite pink nipples and the fullness of her femininity. With a sense of reverence, he caressed her, feeling the weight of her breasts in his hands, running his fingers over the nubs of her nipples, watching them harden and tilt upward.

He looked at her face and saw a soft, vulnerable wince in her eyes. A tear slid down her cheek.

"You're crying," he said, pausing with concern.

She blinked hard and her voice was hushed. "When you touch my nipples, it feels so tender and caring that it makes me emotional." She smiled a bit. "When I trust you with my body, you take such sweet care of me. You must be the best lover in the world."

Kent felt moved by the compliment, but he reminded himself that she had no one to compare him with. He couldn't help but be encouraged that she liked the way he loved her.

As if of one mind, they kissed again. He drew her body against his, enjoying the feel of her mounds of firm flesh pressing into his chest. His sweatshirt was in the way, and he broke the kiss to pull it off. When they embraced again, he almost wept at the intimacy of her silky skin and soft breasts, like satin pillows, sliding against his bared chest.

They kissed and caressed each other until Kent grew so swollen beneath his zipper, he couldn't think straight. They weren't even in bed yet, or completely undressed. But he was afraid to hurry the moment, wanting to take things at her pace.

As she writhed in his embrace, her pelvis moved against him and she looked up and smiled. "You're so big already." Her voice was like honey. She began unbuckling his belt. "Let's hurry. I want you, too."

He impulsively took her by the shoulders and kissed her with playful passion. "You're such a sexy woman!"

The belt undone, she unzipped his pants. "Can't call me shy anymore, can you?"

They laughed and as he removed his clothes and shoes, she undressed herself, both in a delighted frenzy to be one. When they were naked, they fell into each other's arms with eager anticipation. They were about to kiss, but then she hesitated.

"We should use a—"

"I don't have one," he said, alarmed that they would lose this opportunity for lack of protection.

"I do. Remember, I'd bought them? I'll get it."

As she ran off to the bathroom, Kent recalled that last time they both had been prepared. He was glad she remembered to use a condom. They had no commitment yet, though in his own mind he felt committed. In any case, it wouldn't do for her to get pregnant. They weren't married. But he hoped that was a situation that wouldn't last much longer.

She rushed back with a small packet in her hand. "All set," she said, a look of wonder and anticipation in her brown eyes as he took the packet from her. As he applied the sheath, she watched him, a soft new glow of desire shining in her eyes.

Kent was thrilled to see that she was as excited as he. Quickly they walked together to the daybed. After throwing off the pillows, she lay down, face up and opened her arms to him. He slid over her and gently settled his weight on her body. They began kissing and stroking each other until his arousal was so taut, he couldn't control himself much longer. She seemed to sense his need, indeed seemed to feel the same urgency. Without a word, she parted her legs and brought her knees up around him. As he slid slowly into her, she closed her eyes and whimpered with joy. Kent understood how she felt—the sensation of becoming one with her was so warm and comforting that his eyes glazed with tears.

He began to undulate his body in a satisfying back-and-forth motion that brought an erotic groan from them both. But as they kissed hotly the satisfaction turned into urgent need again. Driven by the fierce longing for satiation, he began to thrust harder and faster. She responded with excited gasps and sweet moans that turned him on even more.

"You're so sexy," he whispered, digging his fingers into her tousled short hair as he kissed her mouth. Her body, so soft and pleasurable beneath him, began to writhe with such intense passion that they had to break the kiss. She arched her neck back as she cried out with aching need. And then as he kissed her throat, he felt her body convulse uncontrollably in the throes of her climax. As she called out his name with excited joy, his own body reached the point of no return. He panted and held her tightly until the exquisite pulsing ebbed away and serene satiation made his body relax and grow limp.

After several long moments, he pushed himself off of her and stretched out beside her, pulling her close. She leaned against his shoulder, her eyes in a daze, as if mesmerized by the thrill of their erotic encounter and momentarily weak from the energy she'd expended.

Kent was glad he'd made her happy. "Lovemaking is so intense between us," he whispered, still catching his breath. "Almost unbearably beautiful and sexy. It's obvious we were meant for each other." He pushed her damp hair off her forehead. "I love you, Nellie."

As he told her his feelings, he noticed her eyes seemed to come back into focus. Her expression changed. She seemed to grow concerned and then sad.

"What's wrong?" he asked, worried he'd somehow said the wrong thing. He'd thought a declaration of love was what a woman most wanted to hear at this moment, and besides, it wasn't the first time he'd said it. Indeed he'd told her several times.

Tears filled her eyes now and she sat up on the bed, taking the pillow under her head and holding it against her chest, the way a child would hold a teddy bear. "How do you know it's love, Kent?" she asked.

"Isn't it obvious?"

"It may be only sexual chemistry. Just because it's intense doesn't mean it's love."

"How do you know?" he countered. "What experience are you basing that on?"

"I read a few sex manuals," she said.

He chuckled. "Sex manuals?"

"It was when I was studying up on French painters and the Cubs, trying to attract you. I thought if you did want to go to bed with me, I'd better not look like I didn't know how to go about it. One of the books said that some people—even strangers on one-night stands—can have great sex because the chemistry is right. But that's not love."

"Maybe we have both," Kent argued. "There's no doubt in my mind that I'm in love with you. Since you went to such lengths to pursue me, I can only assume that you feel the same about me."

She tilted her head hopelessly, one way and then the other. "Who do you think you love?" she asked. "The Nellie you met a year ago on the candy audit? The Nellie I made you think I was? Or, since I'm not so shy anymore and I look more sophisticated, are you imagining that now I fit your idea of the perfect corporate wife?"

Kent raked his hand through his hair. "I love all three versions," he told her. "They're all different aspects of the same beautiful woman."

She bowed her head and he saw a tear fall from her face onto the pillow. In a moment she sniffed and looked at him. "It's not that I don't think you're sincere. I think you believe you love me, especially right now after being in bed together. But you've had so many different feelings toward me that I can't be confident that you won't start feeling differently again."

"No, I'm settled now. I…" Kent considered telling

her about his father's retirement dinner, and how the speech he'd made about his mother had made Kent see the light. But he remembered that Nellie did not have a good relationship with her own parents. Telling her she reminded him of his mother might not make any sense to her, or might even strike her as a bad omen. "I thought about it a lot and I realized that you were what I wanted all along," he told her simply, hoping it was enough.

"I want to believe you, but..." She shook her head. "This is too painful for me. I've gone through a whole year wanting nothing but you, and because of my own schemes I've spoiled whatever relationship we might have had. You don't know me. I'm not sure I understand you. All we have between us for certain is terrific sex."

She paused and looked at him with sorrow. "I think we shouldn't see each other anymore."

"What—?"

"Kent, I can't do this. If we go on this way, we'll want to keep on making love. And that's too emotionally painful for me, knowing we don't have a real future together. It's better to end it now, before I get so attached I can't go on without you."

"I don't want you to go on without me. I want to be with you forever."

She looked him in the eye and said, "Tell me that a year from now, and maybe I'll believe it. Until then, I don't think we should see each other, except when we run into each other in the lobby at work."

"A year! A whole year apart? Are you serious?"

"Love is serious," she said. "If you love me now, you'll love me then. It's the best test I can think of."

"You claim I don't really know you," he argued. "How am I supposed to convince you I know you well? How can I learn more about you, if we don't see each other? How is spending a year apart any kind of proof?"

Her eyebrows drew together in a troubled expression. It was obvious she had no good reply to his questions. Her face crumpled and she wiped away new tears. "Maybe it's not, but that's what I feel we have to do. Being with you, sleeping with you, makes me want you too much—more than I can bear, not when I can't be sure of you. My head is clearer when we're apart."

Kent felt desolate—and angry. "So what happens now? After what we just shared together on this bed, you want me to walk out and say, 'Goodbye, see you in a year?'"

As if needing to stick to her guns, she firmly nodded, though she seemed too upset to speak.

Kent stared at her dumbfounded. Nellie had driven him wild in bed, and now she was going to drive him nuts! He'd leave since that's what she wanted, but in his mind he knew there was no way he was going to spend a year hoping to get a glimpse of her in the lobby! Besides, he thought, calming down, maybe if they were apart for a while, she'd miss him and change her mind.

"All right," he said, his tone only a bit testy. "Never say I don't give you what you want. I'll leave. But I won't hold it against you if you change your mind about this decision. Changing one's mind can be a sign of growth—I know that from personal experience. You know where I am. Call me or see me anytime."

She straightened up and nodded. "I don't think I'll change my mind, but it's nice of you to be understanding. I really believe this is for the best."

"Right," he said with a polite nod, copying her. "I'll just get dressed and be out of your way."

"Are you angry?" she asked after a moment.

"Now why would you think that?" He zipped up his pants with a swift jerk.

"You are, aren't you? I'm sorry. I didn't want to hurt you."

"You haven't. You think I'm mixed up about my feelings. I think you're mixed up, period. We're at an impasse. You're right, we might as well stand back and logically assess our situation."

"Y-yes, that's what I mean," she said, sitting on the edge of the bed now, still holding the pillow. "I'm sorry it's happened this way, but I think it's all we can do now."

"Okay," he said lightly as he pulled on his sweatshirt. He grabbed his jacket from the kitchen. When he came back, he found her standing, still clutching the pillow.

"I'm sorry, Kent," she apologized again.

He drew in a breath and let it out in a long exhale. "It's not your fault or mine. Love just got complicated for us, that's all." He managed a little smile. "I'm confident that even this will be resolved."

She looked puzzled and doubtful, as if wondering how he could make such a positive statement.

Let her wonder, he thought. He walked up to her. "Should we kiss goodbye?"

She backed away a step, her fingers gripping the pillow as if for protection. "I don't think we should," she whispered, a renewed glaze of moisture in her eyes.

"Afraid we'll wind up back on the bed?" he asked, raising his eyebrows with patience.

She nodded.

"Well, then this is goodbye," he said.

"Bye." Her mouth formed the word more than actually said it.

Kent went out the door and closed it. As he walked down the hall of her building, he hoped she would call him back, but she didn't. By the time he was heading down the sidewalk toward his car, parked on a side street, plans were already forming in his brain. Kent hoped Nellie would change her mind and phone him. But, knowing how determined she could be from having been pursued by her, he couldn't count on her having a change of heart. He knew she loved him. He knew he loved her. It was only a matter of convincing her. He had an idea how he might manage it.

Nellie had a sister. He'd seen Jeannie Brown just the other night on a TV commercial. It had surprised him that the athletic shoe company that sponsored the commercial was a client of an advertising company that was a client of Kent's. He wondered if he could pull a few strings and manage to get in touch with her. Jeannie Brown might just be his key to success.

## 9

When Kent got home after leaving Nellie's apartment, the first thing he did was call a real estate woman he'd spoken with several times over the last few months. He inquired about a house in Elmhurst on which he'd already made two offers that had been refused. The owners kept asking for a sum that was beyond what he felt he could afford, and was also more than the house was worth in its present state.

"If I go up another fifteen hundred dollars, would the owners go for it?" he asked Mrs. Keller. "I know they're stubborn about their selling price, but would you see how they respond?"

"Be glad to," she said.

She telephoned him a half hour later. "They said if you go up two thousand dollars, agree to accept the old stove and fridge and a close of escrow in fifteen days, it's a deal."

Kent could barely contain himself. "Really? I accept! We've got a deal!"

Mrs. Keller laughed. "Great. Just between you and me, I think they've finally realized their asking price was too high. They're just about to move to their new place in Arizona, too. It's a nice house, but you'll probably want to do some upgrading and redecorating.''

"Fine. I'll redecorate. I want it.''

Kent drove out to the suburbs late that afternoon to sign the appropriate papers. The previous owners were moving out next week, he learned.

On Sunday, he made plans to put his condo up for sale. On Monday morning, he phoned his client who was an advertising agent and asked for a favor. By late Monday afternoon, he had the phone number of a hotel in Paris, France, where Jeannie Brown was staying.

Late that evening he telephoned Paris, hoping he wouldn't be waking up Nellie's sister, for it was morning there. On the other hand, he wanted to catch her before she went out for the day.

"Hello?" a sleepy voice said. *"Bonjour?"*

"Hello, is this Jeannie Brown?"

"Yes.''

"You don't know me. I'm Kent Hastings, calling from Chicago.''

"That name sounds familiar...''

"I know your sister—''

"For heaven's sake! Kent! Nellie talks about you all the time.''

Kent couldn't help but be pleased. "She does?''

"Yes. Did she give you my number?''

"No.'' Kent took a few minutes to explain the roundabout way he'd gotten the name and number of her hotel. "I'm calling because I need your help. I'd like to know everything you can tell me about your sister. Her likes, her dislikes, her pet peeves... everything.''

"This'll be a long phone call. Can you narrow it down a little? And why?"

Kent gave her a detailed rundown of their on-again-off-again romance. "Now she's saying she doesn't think we should see each other, and I need ammunition to win her back. I'm trying the same tactics she used on me."

"This is adorable!" Jeannie gushed. "I love it. Sounds like you're as crazy about her as she is about you."

"I hope she is," he said, worried.

"Oh, she's just sorting things out, I'll bet. Love is confusing. I know. I thought I'd met Mr. Right, and he's turning out to be Mr. Wrong. I tend to rush into things, but Nellie has always been conscientious and prone to doubt. She hoped everything would go perfectly between you and her, and when it didn't, then she probably assumed that everything was terribly wrong. And I suppose she feels guilty about chasing after you. I encouraged her, you know. Though I didn't know she'd bought a book. Poor thing. She probably feels awful. Probably can't believe that you could still love her."

"I've told her I do. I've insisted that I forgive her. But she thinks I'm confused."

"Oh, Nellie, Nellie. What'll we do with her? Let's see, what do you need to know? Her favorite things?"

"That's a good start," he said.

"She loves music boxes. She's been saving up to buy one of those expensive Swiss ones that you can insert disks to play different tunes. Those snow globe ones always intrigue her, too. She has a small collection of them. By the way, her birthday's in six weeks. March 5.''

Kent quickly wrote that down. ''Thanks for telling me. So about the music boxes—what are her favorite songs?''

Jeannie spent the next couple of minutes trying to recall names of songs, and Kent wrote them all down.

''I think her favorite melody is Greensleeves, and she doesn't have a music box that plays it. I remember her saying she keeps looking for that.''

''This is terrific,'' Kent said as he scribbled. New ideas came to him. ''I'm buying a house. She doesn't know yet. What sort of decor does she like? I don't know much about decorating. What about colors?''

''You're going to surprise her with a house?'' Jeannie asked brightly.

''That's my plan so far. I hope she'll like the idea of living in the suburbs and taking the train to work.''

''I don't see why she wouldn't. In fact, if she doesn't marry you, she's nuts!'' Jeannie paused. ''You do want to marry her. Have I misunderstood?''

''Yes, yes, I want to marry her! You think a house would convince her?''

''It would convince *me*. But Nellie's the picture of caution. I admire her for being sensible, but sometimes she thinks too much and she gets in her own way. Well, we'll just have to make it the best house in the world! Let's see. Color—she's an Autumn, so—''

''An Autumn?''

''You know, the color charts? No, being a man, I suppose you wouldn't. Several years ago it was kind of a fad. You'd go to an expert who could tell you which season you fit into. She and I went and had our colors done together when we were in high school. It turned out she's an Autumn, which was interesting, because her color chart showed all her favorite colors. Rust, brown, green, yellow.''

"But she usually wears gray suits to the office," Kent argued.

"Because she read some dress-for-success book that said people expect an accountant to look sort of drab. It recommended gray suits for female accountants."

Kent began laughing. "Isn't that just like her? She buys a book for everything! Though, you should see her lately. She's cut her hair short, and her clothes seem to be livening up. Come to think of it, she has been wearing fall colors."

"Cut her hair?"

"She looks great."

"Well, you see? She's coming into her own. She'll come around. Okay, so now you know her favorite colors. As far as decor, I remember at Christmas at our parents' she and I were looking at catalogs. My mom gets lots of them. Nellie seemed to like the American folk art look."

"Never heard of it."

"Go to an interior decorator or a good furniture store and ask them to show you wallpapers and accessories in that style. You'll get the idea."

Kent felt a little overwhelmed. "I'll see what I can do. How much longer will you be in France?"

"Another three or four weeks."

"Oh," he said with a sigh. "Guess I'll have to do all this myself."

"Call me whenever you want. I'll be pleased to give whatever advice I can. I want her to be happy. And if you're willing to go to this much trouble to win her, then I know you'll make her happy. I'll be your cheerleader, but you'll have to make the plays."

"Thanks. You've given me a lot to do already. I'll call and keep you posted."

Kent went to work. He made a stop at a furniture store and wound up spending hours with an interior decorator there who showed him wallpapers, draperies, pictures for the walls, floor coverings and furniture, until his head was spinning.

The next day, on lunch hour, he went to a shop that specialized in music boxes.

A few weeks later, when the previous owners of his new home had moved out and escrow had closed, he hired painters to paint the exterior of the two-story wood-frame house. He had the linoleum ripped out of the kitchen and bathrooms and had ceramic tile installed. The refrigerator and stove were replaced with ultramodern appliances. He had new rugs installed. But then he grew worried about doing too much to the place without Nellie's approval.

He moved out of his condo and into the house as planned, however. If Nellie was going to live there, he was one fixture she'd have to make do with.

The weeks flew by fast. All at once, it was the beginning of March. Time to go into action. The thought made him nervous and he had trouble eating the evening of March 4. He'd deliberately stayed out of Nellie's way and hadn't talked to her since the day they'd last made love. How was she going to react when he approached her tomorrow? He hoped he wouldn't have to go on living at his spic-and-span new house all alone.

Nellie finished straightening up her desk at the end of the day with a sigh. It was March 5. She was twenty-five. In another five years she'd be thirty. Would Kent still be out of her life then? And would she still be sad and lonely, wishing she hadn't told him to stay away even though he'd forgiven her and wanted her back?

Six weeks had passed since she'd seen him, and he hadn't tried to contact her. She hadn't even seen him in the lobby. When she'd told him they should stay apart for a year, she'd meant it. She'd been upset and didn't know what else to do, how else to be sure of the love he professed for her. After he'd left, she'd sat on the bed hugging her pillow for hours, wondering if she'd done the right thing. By that evening she'd already had regrets about sending away the man she loved.

But she wasn't sure enough of her regrets to go to him and say she'd changed her mind. What if her initial impulse had been correct? People always said you should follow your instinct, and her first instinct, after making love with him again, was that she and he were too close to the situation to know their true feelings. She still feared they might be mistaking an overwhelming sexual attraction for love.

That night she'd comforted herself with the thought that, knowing Kent, he probably wouldn't abide by her request. He'd try to see her again somehow. When he did, her year-apart edict would be forgotten.

But that hadn't happened. He'd actually *stayed*

*away.* Had he decided she was right about the benefits of a separation? Or maybe he'd gone so far as to decide that he was better off without her. Had she lost him forever because of her doubts?

"How come you're looking so glum?" a male voice asked.

She looked up to find Arnie standing near the corner of her desk. "Oh...I'm turning twenty-five today," she confessed to him, mustering a smile. "I'm another year older, but not any wiser."

"It's your birthday?"

"Yes."

"Why didn't you say so? We should have had a cake for you."

"I asked Personnel not to say anything," she told him.

"How about if I take you out to dinner?"

She sighed. "I'd love to, but my mother talked me into coming over tonight. I haven't seen my parents in months. They've got a cake for me, no doubt. And presents."

"Well," Arnie said, "I suppose they have first claim on you—"

"No," another male voice interrupted. "*I* have first claim on her."

Nellie leaned to one side to look around Arnie and saw Kent approaching them. She felt herself turn slightly pale as her heart began to pound. "Kent—"

He stood beside Arnie and looked down at her with a smile. "Happy Birthday."

"How did you know?"

"Just knew," he said blithely. "You're a sight for sore eyes. You look wonderful."

Arnie glanced at one and then the other as they stared at each other. "I can see I'm in the way here," he muttered with glib resignation. "I'll go. But I thought it was all off between you two."

"It is...was," Nellie said, her voice a bit shaky and out of breath.

"It's not," Kent said with conviction, never taking his eyes off her.

"Invite me to the wedding," Arnie quipped with good humor as he walked away.

"It's not?" she asked Kent, ignoring what Arnie had said.

"Nope."

"I thought...I haven't seen you in...I assumed—"

"Never assume. So you're glad to see me?"

Nellie paused. She ought to at least pretend to stand by her convictions. "Yes, but you've broken our agreement."

"It's your birthday. I thought that was a good excuse."

She didn't know what to say, didn't know why he was here, what he hoped to accomplish. "I appreciate the thought. But...we did agree not to see each other. Don't you think we should stick to that?"

"No."

His blunt answer stymied her. "But...we decided..."

"It was your decision."

"You agreed to it."

"Under duress," he said.

"Duress?"

"I was afraid you might cut me out of your life

forever if I didn't agree to a year's separation. But a year's too long, Nellie.''

"You managed pretty well for six weeks," she said, unable to keep a hint of injured feelings out of her voice.

Kent quickly picked up on it. "You mean, you missed me?"

"I...no, I...well, yes, but that's not the point."

"What's the point?" he asked.

"How can we have a dependable relationship if we can't stick to our agreements?"

"A dependable relationship depends on lots of contact and communication with each other. Being separated for a year doesn't do much to facilitate communication, does it?"

Of course, he was right. But Nellie was loathe to admit his argument had logic. "We were getting too emotional...too sexual, to have a clear idea of what we were doing."

"We were falling in love. Emotion and sex are part of the bargain. We should experience those feelings more, not less."

He was doing it again, sweeping her off into uncharted territory before she could even find a map. "But our history together has been so precarious, Kent, we have to...to take things slowly and examine where we are and where we're going."

Kent sat on the edge of her desk. For the first time she noticed he had a small gift bag with him. The silvery bag frothed with coiled white and silver ribbons. She looked away, pretending she hadn't noticed it. But she was dying to know if the gift was for her, and if so, what it was. Kent had never given her a gift before.

"I agree," he said amiably. "Not about taking things slow, necessarily, but about examining where we're going."

She chewed her lip. "Where *are* we going? I mean, where do you think we're headed?"

"Out for dinner?" he asked with a smile.

She shook her head. "I'm supposed to go to my parents' house."

"What time?"

"Seven."

He looked at his watch. "It's five-fifteen. Can you call and tell them you'll be late? Or...tell them you can't make it for dinner, but you'll be there around eight for the cake and so on."

Nellie found herself in a quandary. Naturally she was tempted to go with Kent, to learn what he had in mind, and just to be with him again. But her parents probably wouldn't take it well. For months, she'd been inventing excuses to put off visiting them. When she'd finally agreed to see them on her birthday, her mother had sounded unusually excited, even relieved. It was almost as if she'd worried that Nellie was becoming alienated from them. Her mom's reaction had made Nellie feel better—perhaps her parents did love her after all. Not as much as they did her sister, but maybe they really cared about her, too, in their way. And now, to have to tell them she wouldn't be there until late...

"Call them and ask," Kent urged her.

She drew a long breath. "All right." After dialing, the phone rang.

"Hello?"

"Hi, Mom. Um, something's come up. I can't get there till about eight o'clock. Do you mind? Just go ahead and eat without me. I'll come by and have cake with you later."

"All right," her mother said cheerfully. "Come by when you can. See you then."

"Bye," Nellie said as she heard the phone click. She hung up and looked at Kent. "Well—she sure didn't have any problem over that!"

"Great. Let's go," Kent said, standing up.

Nellie got up from her chair, feeling confused. Her dinner plans for the evening had gotten turned all around, and her mother didn't even care. And now she had Kent to deal with. She was thrilled to be near him again, but what did he want? Just to see her on her birthday? Would he want to continue where they'd left off? Should she get involved with him again so soon? If she allowed him even to kiss her, she'd be back where she was, ready to swoon with love for him. But was it real? He always seemed so sure of himself, but did he really know his own mind and heart? Did he know yet who she was?

Nellie was surprised that instead of using public transportation, Kent escorted her to his car in the building's underground parking garage. He drove her to a new, very "in" restaurant on the Near North Side. They ordered from the menu. She looked around at the avant-garde decor, commenting on the modern art combined with indoor potted trees and Victorian-style draperies. When she turned to face Kent again, she found the gift bag he'd been carrying sitting on the linen place mat in front of her.

She smiled. "What's this?"

"A birthday present."

"Thank you. You want me to open it?"

"Go ahead."

Inside the decorative bag she found a wrapped square box hidden in tissue paper. After removing the paper, she opened the box to find a snow globe inside.

"Oh, gosh, I love these!" she exclaimed, looking through the swirling white "snow" to see an adorable teddy bear holding a red heart in his arms.

"It plays a tune," Kent told her. "Wind it up underneath."

She found the knob and turned it several times. The music box played "Greensleeves." "I've been looking for...how did you know?" she asked with astonishment.

Kent looked pleased, even smug. "I know everything about you."

She laughed. "You do? How?"

"You had your ways. I have mine. You can't say to me anymore that I don't know who you are. And you know what? You're damned fascinating. I've integrated the shy girl I met, the clever woman who set out to please me and the sophisticated C.P.A. you are now, into one magnificent person. And I'm only all the more convinced that you're perfect for me."

Nellie was at a loss. She felt flattered. She wanted to believe him. But how could he say all this? On what was he basing these bold declarations?

"Kent, that's sweet. But, really, you haven't been around me for six weeks. How can you know me better?"

"Exactly the point I made before. We shouldn't be apart."

"But," she persisted, "how can you know me?"

"You had your sources," he repeated with an air of mystery. "I have mine."

Nellie racked her brain as to who he could have talked to. "Arnie?"

Kent chuckled. "He doesn't know any more about you than I. Why would I go to him?"

"Well, who?"

He leaned toward her over the table. "Never mind," he said quietly. "Just know that I think you're perfect...that we're perfect together."

"You said once that I'd made you believe I was perfect," she reminded him.

"I remember. Now I've convinced myself that you are."

Nellie looked down at the snow globe and shook her head. "Kent, what is there about me that you think is so perfect? I lied to you."

"You also confessed. Stop feeling guilty about that."

"But I have lots of flaws you can't even imagine."

"I know. One flaw is that you doubt yourself too much. But it's a flaw I've come to love. You also have a flaw that's similar to one I have—you think too much, try to be logical about emotional issues. I think it's an adorable flaw in you, and I'm trying to accept it in myself. We're more alike than I think you ever imagined."

"But neither one of us is perfect."

"Perfection, like beauty, is in the eye of the beholder," Kent said, taking her hand. "And to my eyes, you're perfect—and beautiful, too."

"I used to think that about you," she said. "Until everything went wrong."

"And you saw me angry and hurt."

"And you saw sides of me you didn't like," she reminded him. "Now we're on some high again, thinking everything's hunky-dory. But, don't you see, it won't last? It didn't before."

"Because we didn't really know each other then, so of course we were in for some rude surprises. But we've learned from our mistakes."

"I wish I could be as confident as you," she said, afraid of believing that Kent wouldn't be disillusioned with her again someday.

"The evening's not over yet," Kent said. "Maybe you will be."

She tilted her head to one side. "What do you mean? How?"

He looked past her and then his gaze settled on her. "The waiter's coming with our food. Let's eat and we'll get into this more later."

"You're awfully mysterious," she said, setting the snow globe aside so that the waiter could lay a salad in front of her.

"Yeah—it's a trait in me you haven't discovered yet. But you'll learn to love it."

"Oh, I will?" she teased.

"Eat," he said with a grin.

She hesitated before picking up her fork. "I don't know if I can," she said with a sigh. "I'm...awfully nervous."

"Being with me again? Or because I'm acting mysterious?"

"Both," she said.

He reached across the table, took her free hand in his and squeezed it. "I'm jittery, too. I had to muster up all the nerve I have to come and see you today. See? Another thing in common. So, let's just try to calm down and eat what we can."

She smiled, tears filling her eyes. "Okay." And then a strange thing happened. Her appetite came back.

They talked about work—Kent's new job responsibilities, Nellie's hopes of being promoted soon— over dinner. As they were finishing dessert, Kent channeled the subject in a new direction.

"You know I got a raise with my promotion," he said offhandedly, scraping chocolate sauce off his plate with a spoon. "I felt I could afford to buy a house, now. I mentioned once that was my plan, remember?"

"Right." She took a sip of iced tea. "So you're going to start house-hunting?"

"I've already bought one."

Nellie set her glass down. "You bought a home?"

"In Elmhurst. Escrow closed almost a month ago. I moved in last week."

"Gosh," she said. "That's great." But, in truth, she felt sad that he was no longer living near her.

"Want to see it?" he asked.

"Sure."

"Good. I'll drive you there after I pay the bill."

"Wait," she said. "I'm supposed to go to my parents'."

He looked at his watch. "It's only a little after seven. We have time for a quick stop."

She wondered if he was using his new home as a ploy to get her into bed and set their relationship into high gear again. "Did you move your bedroom furniture there?"

"Yes. But we...it doesn't have to stay. I don't mind a new set if—"

"You aren't planning to seduce me, are you?" she asked, trying for a joking manner.

He gave her a slow, knowing smile. "Oh, I have plans for you, sweetheart. But seducing you tonight isn't one of them. Strictly platonic, I promise."

Perversely she felt disappointed, then chided herself. They left the restaurant and Kent took the Eisenhower expressway to Elmhurst. It felt odd driving with him to the suburbs. At least Elmhurst wasn't far from her parents' home in Lombard. He'd said he would drop her off there after stopping at his new house. She wondered if she should invite him in to meet her mom and dad. Good grief, what kind of a scene would that be? Her parents weren't used to her bringing boyfriends home. And Kent wasn't an athlete. No, she'd better not invite him in.

Eventually, Kent pulled into the driveway of a white two-story wood-frame house. It looked so crisp and new, she was surprised when he told her it was forty-five years old.

He unlocked the door. "I'm still in the process of redecorating," he said apologetically as he turned on the lights. He held the door open and she walked into the living room.

She smiled as she saw a strip of wallpaper taped

to one wall, and swatches of material taped near the windows. The wallpaper border, taped above, showed a rural drawing of farmland and country houses. The colors were rusts, browns and soft greens on a warm beige background. "I love these colors. This will be beautiful."

He smiled. "I'm glad you like it. I went ahead and papered the kitchen after I had the floor replaced. It's hard to live in a house if the kitchen is messed up." He turned on the kitchen light and led her in.

The carefully finished wallpaper looked wonderful in here with more of the same colors, only a bit more vivid, and the border at the ceiling showed rustically drawn chickens and cows. She turned to him with excitement. "The wallpapers you picked are exactly the type of thing I like. How odd that you happened to choose them."

"Wait till you see the family room." He led her into the next room.

There, taped to the walls, were swatches of another pattern in the same American folk art style and colors. Gosh, she found herself thinking, I'd love to live in this house.

"I have some framed prints on approval from the furniture store." He pointed out several, lined up on the floor against one empty wall. "That one is a Thomas Hart Benton. Next to it is a Grant Wood. The others are by other artists. What do you think?" he asked, looking concerned.

She gazed over the American scenes paintings. "They're all perfect! I love them. It's amazing that you've chosen everything I would pick."

"I wanted to have you look at it, just to be sure,

before I had all the wallpaper put up and the pictures hung.''

"You were waiting for me to look at it?" she asked, puzzled.

"With anxiety," he replied. "I wanted to own a house that you would want to live in. Looks like I've accomplished that."

She took a step backward as her heart rate picked up speed. "You want me to live here? You mean, with you?"

"I wasn't planning to move out."

She brought her hand to the side of her mouth. "I don't think living together is a good idea. At least not just yet."

"I don't mean we should just live together. I mean that we should get married and live here together."

"M-married?" She grew a little faint. This wasn't just another proposal. He'd bought a house and everything. She felt ambushed. Half of her brain told her she should try to escape, and the other half was shouting, *Finally!* But she felt duty-bound to pay attention to the part of her that wanted to escape this foolish man with his beautiful house who thought they could actually be happy here together.

"Married," he said, pulling her into his arms. "Husband and wife. We can ride the train together to work, and come home together and make love."

She shook her head and set the palms of her hands against his chest. "I used to hope you'd want to marry me, Kent. But too much has happened—"

"I know you're stubborn. Or—maybe you're just scared," he said. "It's one thing to dream about marrying a particular person, and another when the reality hits, and that person pops the question.''

"Y-yes, I guess it is," she said in a small voice. Was she scared? She had to admit that what she was feeling was more like fright than anything else. Marrying your dreamboat *was* a scary prospect. They never covered that in the book.

"I've got one more thing to show you," he said. "Upstairs in the bedroom."

He took her by the hand, but she pulled him back. "You promised it would be platonic." She knew if she made love with him tonight, she'd never have the stamina to say no to marrying him, even if it was the sensible thing to do.

"I still promise that," he said.

Nellie wondered what more he had in store for her. "Okay," she agreed with reluctance.

He turned on the light in the bedroom, where the spacious room better fit his oak furniture. He led her to a dresser and pointed to a beautiful wooden box with an inlaid flower pattern.

"This is for you," he told her, "whether you marry me or not. I want you to have it."

"For my birthday?" she asked.

"For just being who you are."

She chewed on her lip, trying not to cry. It was difficult, his words were so touching. She opened the box and discovered the Swiss musical movements inside. And then it began to play "All I Ask of You" from *Phantom of the Opera*.

"Oh, no," she gasped, tears streaming down her cheeks.

"You don't like it?"

"Of course I do. It's the most beautiful thing I ever saw—or heard. But this isn't fair. How can I make a sensible decision about marrying you, when you give me something like this?"

"And it fits so perfectly on this dresser in our bedroom, too," he said with sympathy. "Pretty hard to refuse me, isn't it? I'm really calculating and manipulative, aren't I?"

"No more than I was," she said, allowing him to take her in his arms.

"Another thing we have in common," he said in a jubilant voice. "We're just on the same wavelength all the time, aren't we?"

"Oh," she said, giving him a little shove. "How did you know I loved music boxes? And the songs! You picked the right songs, too."

"Your sister is just as devious as we are. She's the one who clued me in. She told me you were an Autumn and that you liked American folk art. And when I saw what it was, I kind of liked it, too—it has a nice homey quality. And music boxes—well, everybody likes them."

"My sister? But how did you contact her? She's in France."

He nodded. "She was. Time to go to your parents' house."

The thought distracted her. She looked at her watch. "It is? Already?"

"First, I need your answer. Will you marry me?"

"Yes," she said with a sigh that was broken by a little sob. "I just hope we'll be happy."

He smiled. "I think we just might be." He reached

into his pocket and brought out a small velvet jewelry box. "Maybe you should wear this."

She opened it to find a large solitaire engagement ring. "Ohh, Kent, it's beautiful!"

He removed the ring from the box and placed it on her finger. "Now it's official," he said with pride. "We're getting married." He kissed her soundly, then said, "Don't want to be late at your parents'. Let's go."

Taking her by the hand again, he led her down the stairs and out of the house.

He drove her to her parents'. Nellie was so dazed and transfixed looking at her gleaming diamond ring, it was only after he'd parked in front of their house that she realized he already knew how to get there.

As if they'd been watching out the window, her mother and father, Carol and George Brown, opened the front door.

"Hi, Nellie. Hello, Kent," they exclaimed in turns.

"You know him?" Nellie asked them, eyes wide.

"Jeannie introduced us," Carol said with a smile. Her dark brown hair was swept up in her usual French twist.

"Jeannie? She's here?"

Jeannie, dressed in a lavender jumpsuit, stuck her head out the door. "I'm here. Hi, Nellie! Kent, what's the report?"

He gave her a thumbs-up.

"Yay!" Jeannie exclaimed, clapping her hands as if she were a cheerleader.

"I don't get this," Nellie said as they walked into the living room of the house in which she'd grown up. "I feel like I've been set up by my whole family."

"It was Jeannie," her mother said. "We worried that we were losing contact with both our daughters. Jeannie's always traveling and you—you never visit us. When Jeannie returned from France a few days ago, we had a long conversation. She pointed out some things we hadn't realized. We can talk more about all that later," her mother said, giving Nellie a hug. "And then Jeannie mentioned there was this fellow named Kent who wanted to marry you. So I said, 'Will we ever meet him?' She arranged for us to meet, and we all had a nice long dinner here last night. We didn't invite you because Kent had his plans to surprise you with his house and the ring."

"Kent's just right for you, Nellie," her father said, his bald head shining under the ceiling light. The expression in his dark eyes was softer than usual. He almost looked contrite. "He's got your kind of brainpower. It always intimidated me, you know—all those good grades of yours. It's hard to have a daughter who's smarter than her dad. But it's obvious Kent's equal to you."

Nellie smiled, trying not to feel overwhelmed. "Thank you. I'm so happy you think so." She looked up at Kent as she took his hand. "Everything's working out beautifully," she said, feeling so happy she was giddy. "My doubts all seem to have vanished."

"Thank God," Kent said. "You set out to catch me. But you turned out to be the one who's a hard catch. We've finally got that net wrapped around us and I hope we stay tangled in it forever."

"Me, too." Jeannie walked up to them and placed her hands over theirs with obvious affection. "My little sister's getting married ahead of me. Maybe you can give *me* a few pointers on catching a dreamboat!"

\*    \*    \*    \*    \*

## RETURN TO WHITEHORN

Silhouette's beloved **MONTANA MAVERICKS** returns with brand-new stories from your favorite authors! Welcome back to Whitehorn, Montana—a place where rich tales of passion and adventure are unfolding under the Big Sky. The new generation of Mavericks will leave you breathless!

**Coming from Silhouette Special Edition°:**

**February 98: LETTER TO A LONESOME COWBOY by Jackie Merritt**

**March 98: WIFE MOST WANTED by Joan Elliott Pickart**

**May 98: A FATHER'S VOW by Myrna Temte**

**June 98: A HERO'S HOMECOMING by Laurie Paige**

**And don't miss these two very special additions to the Montana Mavericks saga:**

## MONTANA MAVERICKS WEDDINGS
by Diana Palmer, Ann Major and Susan Mallery
Short story collection available April 98

### WILD WEST WIFE by Susan Mallery
Harlequin Historicals available July 98

Round up these great new stories
at your favorite retail outlet.

*Silhouette*®  Look us up on-line at: http://www.romance.net

SSEMMF-J

# Take 4 bestselling love stories FREE

## Plus get a FREE surprise gift!

## Special Limited-time Offer

**Mail to Silhouette Reader Service™**

**3010 Walden Avenue**
**P.O. Box 1867**
**Buffalo, N.Y. 14269-1867**

**YES!** Please send me 4 free Silhouette Yours Truly™ novels and my free surprise gift. Then send me 4 brand-new novels every other month, which I will receive months before they appear in bookstores. Bill me at the low price of $2.69 each plus 25¢ delivery and applicable sales tax, if any.* That's the complete price and a savings of over 10% off the cover prices—quite a bargain! I understand that accepting the books and gift places me under no obligation ever to buy any books. I can always return a shipment and cancel at any time. Even if I never buy another book from Silhouette, the 4 free books and the surprise gift are mine to keep forever.

201 BPA AZH2

| Name | (PLEASE PRINT) | |
|---|---|---|
| Address | Apt. No. | |
| City | State | Zip |

This offer is limited to one order per household and not valid to present Silhouette Yours Truly™ subscribers. *Terms and prices are subject to change without notice. Sales tax applicable in N.Y.

USYRT-296

©1996 Harlequin Enterprises Limited

# Welcome to the Towers!

In January
*New York Times* bestselling author

# NORA ROBERTS

takes us to the fabulous Maine coast mansion
haunted by a generations-old secret and introduces
us to the fascinating family that lives there.

Mechanic Catherine "C.C." Calhoun and hotel magnate
Trenton St. James mix like axle grease and mineral
water—until they kiss. Efficient Amanda Calhoun finds
easygoing Sloan O'Riley insufferable—and irresistible.
And they all must race to solve the mystery
surrounding a priceless hidden emerald necklace.

*Catherine and Amanda*

# THE Calhoun Women

**A special 2-in-1 edition containing
COURTING CATHERINE and A MAN FOR AMANDA.**

Look for the next installment of
THE CALHOUN WOMEN with Lilah and Suzanna's
stories, coming in March 1998.

Available at your favorite retail outlet.

Available in February 1998

# ANN MAJOR

## *CHILDREN OF DESTINY*
*When Passion and Fate Intertwine...*

# SECRET CHILD

Although everyone told Jack West that his wife,
Chantal—the woman who'd betrayed him and sent
him to prison for a crime he didn't commit—had
died, Jack knew she'd merely transformed herself
into supermodel Mischief Jones. But when he
finally captured the woman he'd been hunting,
she denied everything. Who was she really—
an angel or a cunningly brilliant counterfeit?"

**"Want it all? Read Ann Major."**
—**Nora Roberts,** *New York Times*
**bestselling author**

Don't miss this compelling story
available at your favorite retail outlet.
Only from Silhouette books.

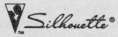

*Silhouette*®

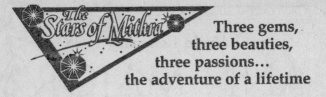

*The Stars of Mithra*

**Three gems,
three beauties,
three passions…
the adventure of a lifetime**

SILHOUETTE·INTIMATE·MOMENTS®
brings you a thrilling new series by
*New York Times* bestselling author

*Nora Roberts*

**Three mystical blue diamonds place three close
friends in jeopardy…and lead them to romance.**

In October
**HIDDEN STAR (IM#811)**
Bailey James can't remember a thing, but she knows
she's in big trouble. And she desperately needs private
investigator Cade Parris to help her live long enough to
find out just what kind.

In December
**CAPTIVE STAR (IM#823)**
Cynical bounty hunter Jack Dakota and spitfire
M. J. O'Leary are handcuffed together and on the run
from a pair of hired killers. And Jack wants to know
why—but M.J.'s not talking.

In February
**SECRET STAR (IM#835)**
Lieutenant Seth Buchanan's murder investigation takes
a strange turn when Grace Fontaine turns up alive. But
as the mystery unfolds, he soon discovers the notorious
heiress is the biggest mystery of all.

Available at your favorite retail outlet.